The Amazing Power of Ashur Fine

A FINE MYSTERY

DONALD J. SOBOL

THE AMAZING POWER OF ASHUR FINE

Troll Associates

Published by arrangement with Macmillan Publishing Company.
For information address Macmillan Publishing Company, 866
Third Avenue, New York, New York 10022.

First Troll Printing, 1987

Printed in the United States of America

10 9 8 7 6 5 4 3 2 1

ISBN 0-8167-1049-X

In memory of our son

GLENN STUART SOBOL

1959–1983

CONTENTS

ONE
METHUSELAH

TERROR would come soon. Terror would come with the elephant. But when Ashur opened his eyes, his only sensation was surprise.

He was lying on a concrete bench. Daylight floated above him as a pinkish gray haze among the motionless palms. A moist, warm stillness embraced him.

His mind awakened with a start, but thought faltered. He could not remember how he had come to be sleeping. He had no idea where he was. A few stars clung to the sky. They looked near enough to pluck, as they always did when he was alone.

He was a lanky youth of sixteen, shy and proper. His strong jaw, which his friends said developed from holding his tongue while others bragged, was now slack, his expression baffled.

He sat up and gazed around him. He was in a landscaped plot of clipped grass hemmed in by shrubs and palmetto palms.

Was it dawn or dusk?

If he had slept through the night, Aunt Ruth would be

worrying. He had to find a telephone right away and let her know that he was safe and well.

Except that he wasn't well. The shapes, colors, and details about him were those of familiar objects. Nevertheless, they looked odd. . . .

He rubbed his eyes and picked up a pebble. It did not yield or twitch. Yet, somehow, it *seemed* different.

Something had happened to him. However mysterious, the change was real and could not be rubbed or squeezed away. It was as if the earth had been nudged an inch off course. Nothing—grass or shrubs or palm trees—seemed the same.

A bird called.

A moment later other birds lifted premonitory voices in the distance. Closer in, the gibbons, those aerial acrobats of the animal kingdom, added their territorial cries. A female gibbon uttered a rising series of *woo-woos*. Ashur had once heard a keeper describe these haunting sounds as the female calling to her lost lover. Quickly two male gibbons gave out matching but higher-pitched cries.

The zoo! He had fallen asleep in the zoo!

He rushed through an opening in the bushes and immediately had his bearings. The area in which he had awakened was the hub. Here the broad entranceway from the ticket booths joined the five narrower roads that curved and interwove among the cages.

Good morning.

The greeting slid into his mind soundlessly. He decided it was his own thought and looked down the road leading southward. The strongest light gathered at his left; it was

2

dawn, then, and not dusk. He had only to wait for the sun. In the daylight everything would be clear.

He wished he knew the exact time, but he had mislaid his wristwatch again. It was somewhere in his room, Aunt Ruth had told him, under a miscellaneous heap of growing pains.

He thought of his wallet. It contained his driver's license. He felt his hip pocket and was relieved by the answering bulge. Whatever else had happened to him, he had not been knocked unconscious and robbed.

Other animals were awakening. They filled the Florida air with the eternal sounds of the African plains. Ashur started down the road toward the lesser apes, the gibbons and siamangs.

The zoo was his special place, though it was cramped, smelly, and outdated. It still had cages to imprison the animals rather than open moats to enclose them. Although Aunt Ruth had taught him to have regard for all men, quite frankly he went on preferring animals, good or bad. Last Sunday he had felt positive that one of the male gibbons, an inquisitive scamp, had actually recognized him.

Come back.

He halted and peered in all directions. The scene sparkled with a peculiar newness, but not a soul was in sight. The animals were silent now. Their cries, which had arisen one by one, had stopped in unison.

The silence was eerie, as eerie as the greeting from the phantom voice and then the command. The animals had quieted as if obeying a master spirit.

A master spirit reigning in a zoo? A phantom voice? Oh,

3

now really, Ashur thought. An overactive imagination, that was the phrase.

He resumed walking, determined to play it cool just once in his life and do as others did, take advantage of an advantage. The animals were his to be with and enjoy, his alone. His private zoo! The opportunity was too rich to waste. The telephone call to Aunt Ruth would have to wait a little longer.

Scarcely had he begun walking than his enthusiasm wavered. It seemed to him that the brimming dawn had spilled goblins behind every corner and bush. He was sure he was being watched.

Despite the plea of common sense, he began casting sidelong glances. Daylight still wore an artificial cast, as if the sky were lined with glass diamonds. Silence, flooding in on all sides, thickened with the tension that precedes some deadly contest.

He was anticipating the voice. When it came again, it was more urgent and more distant.

Come back.

Ashur spun around swiftly, hoping to catch a glimpse of a prankster.

"Where are you?" he murmured.

You shall behold me soon.

"No, let me see you now. Come out and show yourself."

Do not anger me.

"Stuff it," Ashur flung, as loudly as he dared. "Find yourself another hobby."

I have warned you.

"And I warn *you*," Ashur retorted. "Go and pick on somebody el—"

4

His body shuddered from head to toe and seemed to wither. He howled and clawed at his temples. The pain lasted long enough to eject the idea of a prank.

Come.

With a slow, unnatural walk, Ashur retraced his steps to the landscaped plot where he had spent the night. From there he was drawn onto the road that wound past the rhinos, hippos, and elephants. He was abreast of the hippos' enclosure when he received the next command.

Just a little farther.

Ashur stopped. He was too weak to move another step. The voice let him be, and of his own free will he rested his forearms on the guardrail. He was wild to turn his head and see whoever, *whatever*, was doing this, but he was afraid. Any unbidden act might be punished by another flash of pain.

Directly before him stood the hippo enclosure. Like the other large animals, the hippos were confined to their night house. Ashur tried to picture them. Although they were out of sight, he knew they lolled or slept not a hundred feet from him. They existed, proof that the zoo was real.

Ashur drew courage from the hippos, just as he had years ago from his pets. A puppy at his side had been enough. Its presence enabled him to rout the monsters that his imagination had hidden in the darkness under a bed or behind a closet door hanging a slit ajar.

Suddenly, off to his left, from the direction of the elephant barn, wood splintered in a crash that shocked the stillness. Startled bird squawks drilled skyward and spent themselves.

The strange hush settled over the zoo once more.

Ashur clutched the guardrail with barely enough strength

5

to support himself. He stared at his hands, grown pale, and was ashamed of his fright.

Another crash sounded, better defined than before. The noise pealed out like a double thunderclap, as though the door of the elephant barn had been rammed off its hinges and smashed against the ground.

The door was behind the barn, away from public view. Ashur didn't need to see it. He knew the door was down. Whatever had been trapped inside the barn was now *outside*.

He waited, his heart a hammer in his chest.

He had to find out. He drew a nerving breath and twisted his neck. A bull elephant stood by the bars. Ashur recognized Methuselah, the zoo's lone African.

Larger and stronger than their Asian cousins, the Africans were also fiercer and harder to train. Methuselah was that and more. He was moody and unpredictable, and so old that his years were the subject of dispute. At night the Asian elephants were chained inside the barn by one leg. Methuselah was chained by two.

A few links dangled from each of his hind legs. Ashur gazed in disbelief. What born on earth could horrify such a giant? What had panicked him into jerking apart steel chains and crashing down an iron door in order to escape?

Nothing else was to be seen in the elephant yard; nothing was to be heard. Only Methuselah. . . .

Ashur understood. Methuselah had not shrilled the challenge typical of an elephant made anxious. The big bull had not fled; he had crossed the width of his enclosure swiftly and with absolute silence, seven tons moving not fearfully but purposefully.

He was drawn up less than twenty feet from Ashur, facing him at a slight angle. Only one of his eyes was visible; it was partly closed. The lid drooped as if the huge brain behind it—a brain four times the weight of a man's—had momentarily forsaken its physical self.

Then, all at once, there was a stir in the enormous head. The long lashes flickered.

The eye opened wide, a tiny wet pane of amber embedded in the wall of wrinkled skin; an eye like the eye of an idol, glowing with ancient secrets.

The eye rolled and trained itself on Ashur.

I have chosen you.

With a hoarse cry, Ashur dropped to the ground. "Oh, no!" he gasped. He fought upright and tried to run. He threw his head and body forward, and his arms churned like a person running at full speed. But his legs were paralyzed, and his feet remained rooted to the same place.

Methuselah turned until both eyes bore into Ashur.

I have chosen you, that you may be my Abram. Obey me, and your reward shall be exceedingly great.

TWO
THE COVENANT

METHUSELAH remained motionless, fixed to the earth like a great graven image. Suddenly the long trunk shifted aside, revealing a mouth flexed in the likeness of a grin.

Must I show you that which I can do?

The threat rang clearly as the amber eyes leeched into Ashur's. Methuselah followed it with a demonstration.

The road under Ashur's feet peeled away. He felt a force snatch him up and take him hurtling back through the eons—back beyond ice and Eden and a universe torn by fire and gas, back to the edge of the black void itself—and in a flit return him to the zoo.

He landed on the same spot from which he had left, and in the same second. He was grasping the guardrail, too emptied to tremble and incapable of judging whether he had actually traveled through time or been bewitched.

Methuselah reunited with him. Once more the current flowed from brain to brain. The elephant sent; the boy received. The mood of domination ceased, however. Communication became gentle, wooing.

On all your visits to the zoo, Methuselah began, *you never passed me near closing time—till yesterday evening. As no other visitors were nearby to bear witness, I held you overnight by a trivial spell. Now, in the privacy of dawn, before the keepers interrupt, I shall make known to you my will.*

I have singled you out because, although you are young, you are attuned. You place your trust in animals more than in humans. You are caring and unselfish. You will not rebel at putting others before yourself if the cause is just and good. That is your mission, to do good. You shall see to the safety and well-being of all the animals, those of the field and those of the wild, those of the air and those in the waters below.

The thought-patterns dwindled. After a lull, they bunched and issued with renewed vigor. *Here and now it starts. Today you shall receive a small task and the power to accomplish it. In the months to come, you must return to me, to this same spot, and report how you have fared. If I am pleased, a greater power shall be granted you.*

As a token of my trust in you—and should you question that I wish you to do only good—the power today shall be granted before the task is given. Compared to the wonders reserved for you, this first power scarcely amounts to a sleight of hand. You have but to name—

Communication stopped. And before Methuselah could define the power, a horrendous din ripped through the thought-patterns, shattering them into a meaningless jumble of impulses.

In the enclosure alongside Ashur, the hippos were bellowing crazily. Their night house quaked as bodies and hooves beat violently against the cement-block walls.

9

The noise had wrecked Methuselah's control. Ashur was released. Acting instinctively, he whirled and sped from the madness.

Come . . . back.

The elephant had mustered his thought-patterns and sent them weaving through the uproar. They searched out Ashur and tugged at him, futilely. They were no longer reins of authority. Ashur shrugged them off.

He scrambled over the gate at the entrance to the zoo, landed neatly on the balls of his feet, and raced for the visitors' parking lot.

The lot was empty except for his pickup truck, which was parked at the south end. The fenders sagged. Rust blistered the cheap, yellow repaint job that had been slapped on by a previous owner. But today it didn't matter. The shabby truck would whisk him home to reality.

The traffic light switched down to green, and the sights outside the windshield leaped at him. Deserted shop fronts stroked by, mutely washed in blank, shadowless glare by the rising August sun. He passed Carney's hardware store, which was about eight miles from the zoo. Eight miles. . . . He had driven eight miles with no recollection of the trip.

At South Forty-eighth Street he turned right. The film that had bedeviled his vision since he'd awakened had dried off. After twelve blocks he took another right. He was home, a six-room house, white with black shutters, and an overgrown lawn.

"Did you sleep?" Aunt Ruth asked. She was seated in the kitchen with her arms crossed over her bosom, as if straining to hold herself in.

"I slept at the zoo," Ashur replied.

The lines around Aunt Ruth's eyes deepened. She used her wrinkles to express small disapprovals. "I'll fix you an omelet," she said, slipping to her feet.

Ashur retreated to his room, which Aunt Ruth referred to either as a "curiosity shop" or a "junkyard clone." The choice depended on how recently he had fulfilled the whim to see a yard of naked carpet.

For a change Ashur's room did not need picking up, except at the foot of the bed where, by sheer luck, Thursday's socks, shorts, and shirt had landed together in style. The contours and textures modeled a free-form sculpture. For several seconds he gave himself over to admiring the masterpiece. Then he demolished it in the bathroom hamper and made his bed.

Despite its shipshape order, the room retained his personality. Tapes, science-fiction paperbacks, and catalogs from Cornell and Yale crowded the bookshelves, pressing against one another as if seeking his attention. The desktop was stacked with nature magazines dating back two and three years, and as browned and crinkled from handling as bark.

Posters of cars, vocal groups, and wildlife busied the walls. Above his pillow hung a group portrait of four cow elephants and a baby. He postponed what he had to do by fussing with the bedspread, smoothing crevices into ridges and ridges back into crevices. Eventually he nerved up to it. He untaped the elephants—they had been his favorite poster. He rolled it into a white scroll and, fingers tingling, stood it in the closet behind his baseball uniform. Calming himself with a shiver, he walked back into the kitchen.

11

Breakfast was on the white-and-gold Formica table. As he sat down, Aunt Ruth said he looked pale. "Did you sleep well last night?"

"Pretty well. The animals didn't snore," Ashur replied. Using a flap of omelet, he dammed up his mouth against further conversation.

Aunt Ruth turned her face to the window. She dipped her hands into the pockets of her pink housecoat as though putting away the desire to know more.

Ashur had rinsed off his plate and was fitting it into the dishwasher when she spoke again. "It's Saturday. Don't forget to bathe Winkie."

"Is he in the house?" Ashur asked, surprised. He had missed the little dog's greeting when he came home.

"He got out when I fetched the newspaper," Aunt Ruth said. "He's probably at the Carters'. I'll bet that's where he picked up the fleas."

Ashur took down a box of borax soap for Winkie's flea-bath and a bag of bread crumbs for the goldfish. He went to the Florida room first. Sprinkling pinches of crumbs into the aquarium, he watched for Big Fellow's hungry charge. The old goldfish darted to the surface on cue—and did something extraordinary. He veered off and dived among the plants. The other goldfish joined him, twisting and bumping in agitation. The bread crumbs sank, untouched, to the bottom.

Winkie did not run away. The little dog stood in the washtub and submitted to the soaping with an air of trust and devotion. All the same, he did not once look directly at Ashur and had not done so since being brought home for the flea-bath. At the sound of Ashur's calls, the dog had bounded

12

joyfully down the street. Drawing close, he had lowered almost to the ground and crept the last few feet, as though he saw something invisible to Ashur.

Ashur toweled him off, being careful of the sorest spots, the throat and rump. Here the hair had thinned and the flesh was bitten pink.

"Same time next week, sport?" the boy asked affectionately.

The little dog turned half away and sat down. He stared at his front paws as if there were no other place that was safe to look.

The bathroom mirror reassured Ashur. He had not changed into a demon that scared goldfish and dogs. No fangs curved over his lower lip; no slime oozed from his cheeks. The face in the mirror was his, which, though to his relief at the moment, was not entirely to his everyday liking. His features seemed to be competing with each other for growing space. Yet they had an appropriate air of modesty, as if they knew that in three or four years they'd team into looks of unapologetic manliness.

"I'm leaving now," Aunt Ruth said from the bathroom doorway. She wore her Naive Old Lady disguise: a floppy hat, sneakers, and mismatched skirt and blouse. Binoculars hung from her neck. "I'll take Winkie. Good luck in the ball game this afternoon."

"You're not into something dangerous?" Ashur asked.

"No, just your basic legwork," she replied. "I've got a gift for one Otto Lindt, a subpoena. He saw an accident and he's wanted as a witness. For some reason he's afraid to testify. He's hiding out on South Sixth Street."

She kissed Ashur a quick good-bye, tugged her hat to its silliest angle, and said, "Don't forget, hit one for me."

The front door clattered shut, and Ashur was left to worry about her. As a private investigator, she'd been cursed and chased, but so far never beaten up. He wished she would carry a gun. He had pleaded with her many times, but she wouldn't hear of it. "I'm not a law enforcement officer," she'd say brusquely.

Her weapons were binoculars, notebook, and Winkie. No one suspected an innocent bird-watcher or a harmless biddy hunting a lost dog. Today she'd inquire, "Otto Lindt, did you see that robin?" Or, "Otto Lindt, did you see my dog?" Before he'd said more than no, and wondered how she knew his name, the subpoena would thwack in his hand. "I'll be damned," he'd say.

Knowing Aunt Ruth's professional ability helped lessen Ashur's concern. She loathed violence; she never courted danger. "I'm not the stuff heroines are made of," she guaranteed him.

Ashur had three hours before the baseball game. He flung himself into his Saturday chores. By working feverishly, he hoped to fend off memories of Methuselah and the uncompleted command to "do good." Do good for whom? For the ancient and mysterious beast?

He cut the lawn, trimmed the hedges, and raked the pine needles from the driveway. He packed everything into three green garbage bags and set them by the curb for Tuesday's trash pickup.

He felt better after he'd showered. He had worked off most of his fear.

14

He had half convinced himself that the encounter with the elephant was a nightmare. When he'd awakened this morning, the unexpected sight of the zoo, stage-lit by dawn, had provided a fertile setting for the nightmare to extend itself. It had held onto his sleep-fogged mind. Yes, that was the explanation. The realistic dream and the dreamlike reality had fused. In running to his truck, he had fled from nothing more menacing than a bad dream.

On the drive to the ball field he stopped for four dollars' worth of gas. He had a happy-headed sense of liberation. An elephant's slave? Not likely. He was himself again, a sixteen-year-old orphan, a high school senior who hoped to study forestry at Yale or veterinary medicine at Cornell.

He drove toward the ball field.

The morning was ending. He would later remember it for what it was, his last hours as only one human being, as a boy named Ashur David Fine.

THREE
WELCOME BACK, BABE RUTH

AT the American Legion Park, the Bears were into their pre-game warm-ups. Ashur joined the outfielders.

Coach Pardee glowered as Ashur trotted onto the field. "You're late, Fine. Let me see you move your butt!" the coach bawled, and fungoed one a country mile.

Ashur moved, feet gliding low to the grass. He seemed to be loafing till he reached up into the sunshine. The ball arched downward and sank snugly into his glove.

He tossed in and glanced warily at the wooden stands behind first base. Darlene Morrison was in the front-row seat she occupied whenever the Bears—and Rod Coglin—played. She had lively blue eyes and honey-colored hair, and her beauty made her smallest quip unforgettable.

To Ashur, the girls of Northeast High School were divided into two groups. In one group were all the rest of the girls, the pretty and the homely, the bright and the dull, all of them an inch on either side of ordinary. In the other group was Darlene—alone, tall, beautiful, and with no human weaknesses of any kind. He wondered if she had noticed his catch

16

and what it must be like to win a goddess.

The Cubs took over the field, and Coach Pardee gathered the Bears around him. A muscular man, he taught shop in junior high school, where he spoke softly. As a coach in the summer league for sixteen- to eighteen-year-olds, he spoke in a drill sergeant's baritone.

Ashur liked him, even though the coach had chosen Rod Coglin to be the Bears' first baseman. Both Ashur and Rod played the position on their high school teams, Ashur at Northeast, Rod at Cathedral. Rod, being a lefty, could start the first-to-second double play faster, the coach had explained. Ashur had accepted the decision and had gone to right field, where the team needed him most. The humiliation smarted. Right field was the leftover position, the out-of-harm's-way country to which lummoxes were exiled.

Coach Pardee's pep talk was sanded to essentials. Beat the Cubs today and the Bears would qualify for the regionals in Fort Lauderdale. The boys didn't have to be reminded of the glitter beyond—a trip to the state championships in Tallahassee.

The Bears batted first. The Cubs' pitcher, Mike Silverman, had developed a hop in his fastball since the Bears had beaten him last month. He retired the side without a hit. For the Bears, Billy Erickson matched Silverman almost pitch for pitch. After eight innings, neither team had scored.

Ashur wrested a shade of consolation from the shutout. Rod Coglin, who had started dating Darlene Morrison last month while Ashur was getting up the nerve to ask her out, was hitless. Rod's subpar performance, however, failed to curb his airs. He looked over at Darlene Morrison with a smug

17

expression of ownership on his handsome face. Only a god can win a goddess. . . .

In the top of the ninth inning, Ashur was up third. He took his bat and another and whipped them around briskly, swishing the air.

Jimmy Flannagan walked. Ashur knelt on deck and watched Bob Nichols foul off a change-up.

"Wait 'em out, Bob!" Ashur hollered, his words mingling with the cries from both benches and the stands. He stole a glance at Darlene Morrison. Their eyes met.

"You're overdue, Ashur," she called to him. "Belt one!"

Ashur smiled self-consciously and bowed his head and peered at his knuckles. If he could hit a home run, thereafter and forevermore she would be his. Let Rod Coglin fret and pine with the also-rans!

How storybook and how perfectly cockle-brained—and how Ashur longed for it to be true! The longing winged him to the land of daydreams.

I wish, he thought. I wish I were Babe Ruth. I'd slam a homer over the fence and have every girl in school kissing me. She'd have to wait her turn.

The fantasy of being a game-busting hero so enthralled him that he missed the double play.

Coach Pardee bellowed, "Get with it, Fine. You're up!"

Ashur walked to the plate as the Cubs' bench bombarded him with the old razz. He cast aside the weight bat and looked bemusedly at the one still in his grip. It felt much too light, even though it was his own.

He went back to the Bears' bench, taking mincing steps. He picked up Larry Tucker's bat, the heaviest one on the team.

18

"Okay, go on," Larry said, as if Ashur had asked permission, or all of a sudden didn't have to.

Again Ashur headed for the batter's box. He looped behind the umpire and came around on the left side of the plate.

He was not a switch-hitter. Never in his life had he batted left-handed. And yet batting lefty seemed altogether natural, as if he'd been born a lefty.

His stance at the plate was unlike a mirror image or an adaptation of how he batted righty. His feet were closer together, and he held the bat nearly upright by his shoulder. He felt enormously powerful and unpardonably cocky.

Coach Pardee took a few hasty strides from the third-base coach's box. He cupped his hands to his lips to shout across the infield. Then, seemingly changing his mind, he dropped his hands akimbo and stared at Ashur, as if seeing something or someone vaguely familiar.

Silverman's fastball hissed in knee-high and nipped the inside corner of the plate. It was the kind of pitch Ashur liked to punch between the third baseman and the shortstop. He let it go past for a called strike.

He'll come back with a curve.

The prediction popped into Ashur's mind from some source of baseball experience far greater than his own. He shifted his right foot. . . .

The curve broke in front of the plate and spun downward. The ball appeared freakishly big and clear despite the speed and spin. Ashur *saw the stitching* and swung.

He held the follow-through—hands clutching the bat, torso swiveled, chin lifted—as he watched the gigantic home run soar over the right-field fence. The ball traveled high enough and far enough to rattle the upper tier of Yankee Stadium.

With an amused smile he circled the bases. His weight came down daintily on pigeon-toed feet, while his body stayed stiffly upright like that of a man girdled by a beefy waistline. Coach Pardee applauded him on the seat of his pants as he rounded third. His teammates pummeled him.

A strikeout ended the Bears' half of the inning. They bounded onto the field, eager to protect the one-run lead, and peppered each other with timeworn, rah-rah words of inspiration. Ashur was the last into position. He had to borrow a lefty's glove from the second-string center fielder.

A single put the Cubs' lead-off batter on first base with the tying run. Two infield flies held him there. The Bears rejoiced by holding up two fingers and chanting for the benefit of latecomers and persons who couldn't see, "Two away! Two away!"

The next Cub batter was undoubtedly a good-natured youth, but devoted to winning. He connected to right field. Rod Coglin dived at the line drive and slowed it with the fingertips of his glove.

Ashur scooped up the loose ball in his bare left hand and wristed it to second base. The flip, executed hurriedly and off balance, was harder and more accurate than he could have made right-handed. But it was too late. The runner from first slid in, hooking the bag with his toe a shake before the tag struck his leg. The umpire's armspread signaled safe.

A walk filled the bases, and the security of the Bears' one-run lead tottered. The next Cub batter doubled, scoring the tying and winning runs. Like that, the dream of Tallahassee and the state championship blew out.

Despair under a dazzling sun. The Bears stood around stunned and unable to do a fool thing. After a while Ashur jogged toward the bench. Then he noticed: He was running like his old self.

His legs had been delivered from the mincing, pigeon-toed gait. His feet bounced lightly over the grass, toes pointed straight ahead. His body swayed in tune with his strides and the flexions of his flat, young waist.

He swerved at first base. He preferred Darlene Morrison in the stands to the gloom around the bench. She sat alone, bliss in a pleated skirt, waiting to be carried off in Rod Coglin's blue convertible. Even if the towering homer had fallen short of winning the game, it ought to be good for an experiment, or at the very least a smile.

The smile was there, and above it her brows knit in interest at his approach. The words clotted in his throat. Mercifully, she spoke first. "Congratulations on the home run. Has the ball come down yet?"

"It has, but I haven't," Ashur replied, and he sought in her face a sign of the impression he was making on her. "I want to ask you something."

The honey-colored head lowered as he fished for the right words. He gave up and said it boldly. "I'd like you to throw a baseball with me."

The honey-colored head lifted. The blue eyes danced with merriment. "Where we can be alone together? Just the two of us, throwing?"

"Yes, and it has to be a secret," Ashur said in an earnest, low voice before he realized she was teasing. He felt sure he was blushing crimson.

Rod Coglin called to her impatiently.

"Stay here," she said. Her forefinger pressured his arm as softly as a kiss.

She walked off hurriedly. The sway of her pleated skirt was something Ashur could have watched for hours without tiring.

The conversation with Rod was short. At one point he looked over her head at Ashur, whom he obviously viewed as a momentary inconvenience rather than as a serious rival.

"I'll pick you up at eight," Rod said loudly as they parted. Darlene nodded without turning around.

"*Zippitydoodah!*" she gasped at Ashur. "Is *he* seething. You really heated up his cool."

"I hope you're not in trouble," Ashur said.

"Only if you can't drive me home. I just lost my ride."

"How does a yellow pickup sound?"

"Fine, as long as it moves."

He wasn't sure what she meant. Was he nothing more than a convenient set of wheels? To show that he really didn't care one way or the other, that she was no one special, he grinned and glib-mouthed, "I read you loud and clear."

"Try reading between the lines," she said in a small voice. She looked away, and it was several seconds before she spoke again. "Maybe I'd like to ride with you even if you hadn't socked the longest home run this side of Mars."

"Oh, every girl says that," he retorted lightly. He was still clumsily trying to play the smoothy. Only now he was acting to keep from yelping with joy.

She shook her head gently at him and entwined her fingertips in his. He felt as though the tips of their lips were touching. The loss to the Cubs was suddenly unimportant.

The place Ashur had chosen for the experiment was a glen secluded by Australian pines, behind a little duck pond. Darlene put on his glove. She dipped into a semicrouch and pounded the pocket fiercely. "Put 'er in there, Ashur ol' boy, ol' boy," she urged him in a mock-croaking voice.

Ashur threw left-handed. Before the ball started from his fingers, he knew. The magical strength that had possessed his left arm during the last inning of the game had vanished. His overhand motion was weak and awkward, typical of a righty throwing lefty.

The ball sailed wide and low. Darlene, a softball player, backhanded it nimbly. "Hey, I can do as well as *that*!" she chided. She removed the glove and with her left hand pitched the ball to Ashur. If the wobbly throw was not quite so good as his, it was not much worse.

Ashur let the ball get by him intentionally. He overtook it at the edge of the pines. There, off by himself, he muttered, "All right, here goes." He closed his eyes, blanked his mind, and then thought solemnly, I wish I were Babe Ruth.

He waited anxiously. Blood and bone and tissue prepared to host the abilities of the old New York Yankee slugger. Nothing inside him changed, and hope wound down with each passing second. Neither the mighty physical talents nor the mountainous self-confidence reentered him. He remained Ashur Fine, through and through.

"Can't you find it?" Darlene shouted.

Disappointed, Ashur stopped and picked up the ball. "Catch," he called, and threw to Darlene, right-handed.

At seven o'clock he drove her home, heady from two hours of strolling close, talking, and strolling closer. She lived in a large Mediterranean-style house in a neighborhood where all the homes backed onto man-made canals. The private yachts moored at the seawalls vied whitely with each other for size and gleam.

He saw her to the door. She thanked him for the afternoon and lifted widened eyes to his. It was, he discovered, possible to kiss a goddess on the first date.

As he drove home, he pondered the larger miracle.

Methuselah had bestowed a Power. Ashur was certain of its unearthly effects though ignorant of its limits. He might have been able to do far more than hit and throw left-handed, but the hippos' mysterious pounding and roaring had cut short the giving of the Power. He had received a fragment only. During the game against the Cubs, he had discovered the fragment quite by accident.

In one inning, he had not only discovered and used the fragment, he had used it up.

For a time, anyway, so he believed.

FOUR
THE TWO DARK-SUITS

AS Ashur drove up to his house, he saw a gray sedan standing at the curb midway down the block. He didn't recognize the car. It didn't belong in the neighborhood. Home owners parked off the street.

At the sight of the black-and-white patrol car in his driveway, he forgot about the gray sedan. An officer waited at the front door, a slip of paper pressed against his thigh. Ashur stopped the truck on the grass.

"Ashur Fine?" the officer inquired.

Ashur hesitated, then nodded.

"Your aunt, Ruth Owens, was injured in a mugging this afternoon. They're holding her overnight at Memorial Hospital for observation, a standard practice in such cases."

He had no details. He cut off Ashur's anxious questions with an apologetic shrug that expressed his lack of information better than a string of I-don't-knows.

"Your aunt wants you to bring her some things," he said, and held out the slip of paper.

Ashur read the list with relief. It was written in Aunt Ruth's handwriting. The letters were round and firm and not the least unsteady. Surely that spoke well of her condition. He got the items—housecoat, nightie, slippers, toilet kit, and fresh underwear and stockings—and packed them in an overnight bag. He added a copy of *Billy Budd* from her night table.

"She wants you to pick up her car," the officer said. "She left it on South Sixth Street, near the Gold Star Hotel. I'll run you there."

Aunt Ruth's tan station wagon was easy to spot. Clean and undented, it stood out in the stenchy neighborhood of sick, tired-to-death shops and houses, all lined up as if awaiting treatment by a wrecking ball.

"Thanks for the lift," Ashur said.

"Your aunt is going to be all right," the officer replied. He smiled, jerked a fisted thumbs-up, and sped off.

Ashur had the station wagon going before the patrol car had left his sight. His thoughts skittered ahead to the hospital, and it was a mile or so before he noticed the car tailing him.

Despite the fading light, he made out the color—gray. Was it the same car that he had seen on his street? He flirted with reversing direction and zigzagging, but he held his course. His foremost concern was to get to the hospital and see Aunt Ruth, and as directly and quickly as possible.

Traffic was light. The gray car used it cleverly, dodging behind buses and trucks, and once even turning down a side street and reappearing farther on. The driver either had the patience and skill of a professional, or he had divined Ashur's destination.

The hospital was a mass of soaring white walls. Ashur knew exactly where to hide the station wagon—in the unlighted space beside the entrance to the emergency ward. Aunt Ruth had used the same space when she had brought him to the hospital after he'd fallen out of a tree house on his tenth birthday.

He glided to a stop, turned off the headlights, and watched the gray car slowly cruise by. It passed him behind a double row of vehicles in the visitors' parking lot. Two men were inside.

Ashur acted swiftly. Reaching under the dashboard, he flipped the switches that he had rigged for Aunt Ruth, and that she used on mobile surveillance. One switch killed the interior overhead light and the other the brake lights. She could slip in and out of the car at night unnoticed and back up and stop without lighting the rear of the car. A second pair of switches enabled her to turn off one headlight at a time, giving the station wagon a different appearance through a rearview mirror.

The gray car crept along the rows of vehicles, searching for the station wagon or a spot to stop. Ashur didn't wait to find out which. He darted under the overhang and into the hospital. At the information desk in the main lobby, he obtained Aunt Ruth's room number.

She tried to smile at him and succeeded with a lopsided pull of the lips. The left side of her face was as swollen and discolored as a burst plum.

"I forgot to duck," she said, her words limping and slurred.

Ashur leaned over and kissed her gingerly on the forehead. "A policeman told me you were mugged."

"Punched and mugged," Aunt Ruth corrected. "Whoever did it stole my wallet but left my pocketbook. It was lying in the street when I woke up, and so was I."

"Otto Lindt, the man you were to serve with a subpoena, was he the one?"

"Not unless a seventy-year-old can hit like a Louisville slugger," Aunt Ruth replied. "Besides, he'd need a fifteen-foot reach. I didn't get closer than that when he came out of the Gold Star Hotel. He looked toward me and gave a startled grunt. Then the lights went out."

Ashur drew up a chair. "Didn't he try to help you?"

"I can't say. When I came to, he was gone, but I'm not sure. With your face in the gutter and two of your teeth loose, you don't count the house."

"Why would a mugger bother to fish out your money?" Ashur asked. "Wouldn't he take the pocketbook and run?"

"Running with a woman's pocketbook in your hand wouldn't exactly win you the brightest thief of the year award, now would it?"

"I think Otto Lindt should have tried to help you, or at least called for help," Ashur insisted stubbornly.

"Maybe he did call the police. Someone did." She propped herself on an elbow and sipped water through a straw. "Lindt is a strange bird."

"How so?"

"He didn't want to testify in a traffic case," Aunt Ruth said. "A few weeks ago he happened to be at the scene of an automobile accident. He and an officer who was leaving a coffee shop were the only witnesses. The officer had a hard time getting his name. One car ran a red light, smashed into a car crossing its path, and injured the driver, a young woman. The woman's husband is suing. Apparently Lindt went into hiding rather than get involved."

"I'll bet he has a police record and is wanted for some crime," Ashur said.

"He's as clean as Lady Astor's silverware," Aunt Ruth said. "He told the policeman at the accident that he was retired. Years ago he did some kind of work finding water for farmers out West."

"Locating him at the Gold Star Hotel must have been hard," Ashur observed.

"It took about an hour and a half of telephone calls," Aunt Ruth answered. "Otto Lindt's last address was a hotel on Tenth Street where you buy a night's lodging for the price of a can of roach powder. I figured he'd jumped to another flea-hole. I'm chummy with the staff at most hotels around town. The night clerk at the Gold Star told me a Karl Lindermann had checked in the day after the car accident. When they choose a new name, most people keep the first letter of their last name. Lindermann and Lindt are close. The night clerk's description of Lindermann fitted Lindt button for button. That's all there was to it."

"I'm going to find whoever mugged you," Ashur said with all the determination in him.

"You'll do nothing of the sort," Aunt Ruth retorted. "Mugging is a crime for the police. Listening to me talk for ten years doesn't make you Mr. Sherlock Holmes."

"If only he could help me," Ashur murmured.

"Who?"

"I was just thinking how nice it would be if I could get

Sherlock Holmes to help find the mugger."

"If you must play detective, find Winkie," Aunt Ruth said. "I had him with me outside the Gold Star Hotel. After I woke up, he wasn't anywhere to be seen."

"He'll find his way home," Ashur said. "But I'll look around the hotel at daylight, just to be sure."

Outside the door a nurse called, "All visitors out by eight o'clock, please. You have five minutes."

Aunt Ruth fingered through the afternoon newspaper that lay on her tray table. "This might interest you," she said. "Look at the story on the front page of the second section. About the hippos."

Ashur opened the newspaper with foreboding. The two-column headline at the bottom of the page soared up to his eyes: HIPPOS DIE IN ZOO MISHAP. Before he had read the first word of the story, his hands were trembling.

Four hippopotamuses were found dead at the Flor-ida Zoo early today. Authorities said an elephant killed them.

The hippopotamuses—three adults and a new-born calf—suffocated from the heat and steam after water hotter than 140 degrees poured into their pool, a zoo spokesman said. The water in the pool is normally kept at 68 degrees.

Baffled by the circumstances, the zoo called in detectives. After an investigation, they concluded that a seven-ton giant African male elephant named Methuselah had pulled free of its chains in an ad-jacent enclosure, reached over security fencing, and opened a hot-water valve with its trunk.

An official said that the elephant, whose age has

puzzled experts, has not always been perfectly be-
haved during his thirty years here.

"The animal must have been playing with the
valve," he said.

Ashur tingled with horror. *Playing* with the valve?

The truth was known to him alone. The hippos had protested passing the Power to human hands, and Methuselah
had exacted gruesome revenge.

Ashur folded the newspaper and replaced it on the table
casually, too casually.

"You're taking the news very calmly, considering you're
so fond of elephants," Aunt Ruth commented. She laid a hand
on the newspaper. "What do you think will become of
Methuselah?"

"He'll be moved to another zoo, I suppose," Ashur said,
sounding indifferent. "Or destroyed. Or he might become the
biggest tourist attraction in Florida—a rogue elephant, that
sort of thing."

"I don't know why, but the story gives me the willies,"
Aunt Ruth confessed. "I have this feeling that the hippos didn't
die by accident."

"Animals kill, but they don't murder," Ashur fibbed. He
rose from the chair and bent over and kissed her. "I'd better
be going. Take good care of yourself, and call me when you
know about tomorrow."

"I should be kicked out by noon. Go home, get some
sleep. You suddenly look terribly tired."

"I am," he said, as though his weariness stemmed from
earthly exertions. Even as he kissed Aunt Ruth good-bye, Methuselah remained like a breathing stillness in his brain.

31

An ambulance was drawn up to the emergency entrance, blocking the view from the parking lot. Ashur used the vehicle's concealing length to start the twenty-yard sprint to the station wagon. He had backed out and was traveling forward before he turned on the lights. A mile from home he changed direction. Headlights shone in his rearview mirror and would not go away.

He could not drive home. The two men in the gray car knew where he lived. He had to lose them and find a place to spend the night and try to sort out what it all meant.

He wondered if there was a baseball game at the University of Miami. He might lose himself in the crowd. He followed Route 1 into Coral Gables. The stadium lights were out, the surrounding grounds dark and abandoned.

He cut east two blocks and reemerged onto Route 1. He drove to the nearest crowded area, the Dadeland Shopping Center.

In front of Burdines department store he got lucky. He plugged a space an instant after a convertible vacated it. He didn't look for the gray car. It was there, somewhere, stalking him. He ran for the nearest entrance.

Evening shoppers crowded the main mall. Ashur looked for a group to join and so acquire the cover necessary to escape through a side exit. He was measuring his steps at a pace scarcely faster than a loiter when he noticed a bald man in a dark, tailored suit. The man seemed ill at ease. He was standing beside a tile statue of a dolphin that small children loved to play on. A blunder. No children were nearby to be dandled, cooed at, or chuckled over, and he didn't look like the type to ride the dolphin while his mommy shopped.

There had been two men in the gray car, Ashur remembered.

He turned and faced the double storefront of a musical-instrument shop. A tilt of his head disclosed a second man coming from his right. The man should have looked at Ashur looking at *him*, but he didn't. He had blond hair, and, like the man by the tile dolphin, he wore a dark business suit.

To link the two men was a slap shot. Dark-suit bald might be a doctor and dark-suit blond a lawyer, strangers to each other. Or they might be a pair of funeral directors renewing themselves amid the shove and jostle of the living.

He walked into the music shop.

A poster leaned on a polished easel by the door. To give the dark-suits a minute to go their own ways if strangers or maneuver to team up if partners, Ashur engrossed himself in it.

Now You Can Play

Drums-Brass-Piano-Organ-Guitar

Classical, Folk, Rock, Bluegrass, Pop, Jazz

Group or Private Lessons Available
Inquire at Counter

Customers and lookers mingled inside the store. Teenagers filling time eyeballed the guitars hanging on one wall and the shiny display of snare drums by the sliding glass doors.

Ashur idled up to a group of three men and a woman. A salesman was working industriously to sell them an upright piano for their church social hall.

33

Out of the corner of his eye, Ashur saw dark-suit bald come into the store. He strolled past Ashur and moved on.

He's going to use the rest room, Ashur thought, or he's stationing himself by the back door.

Dark-suit bald didn't enter the rest room. A couple of feet from the rear door he took a book of sheet music from a wall rack and began to study it. Dark-suit blond had lit a cigarette and was seated in the mall on a bench next to a kiosk draped with sunglasses. He had one leg crossed over the other, enacting the role of a long-suffering husband stranded by a shop-hopping wife.

Ashur had no more doubts. They were partners. Between the one in the back of the shop and the one seated in the mall, Ashur was fairly trapped.

The sale of the upright piano dangled. The church members liked the appearance and size of the instrument, but they wanted to hear it played. Unfortunately, the only pianist on the committee was in bed with a summer cold. And as no one on the night staff of the store played anything but the guitar, the bargaining stalled.

"Perhaps I can help," Ashur volunteered.

The committee regarded him blankly. "Do you play?" the woman asked.

"Yes," Ashur heard himself say. "I can play whatever you like."

"Well, by all means, please do," the woman responded. Her invitation blended a pinch of gratitude with an overflow of astonishment at his forwardness.

Ashur, who had never touched a piano keyboard in his life, sat down to play.

34

FIVE
THE CHASE

ASHUR gripped the ends of the piano bench. Instinctively he kept his fingers as far as possible from that frightening stranger, the keyboard.

The three men of the church committee gathered around him, happily believing he could demonstrate the instrument's quality. The woman member, a diet-slender brunette dressed in a suede jacket and floppy tie, faced him from behind the upright soundboard. Her eyes shone with a skeptical, show-me look.

Her hostility was the helpmate Ashur required to play the piano. He smiled at her stupidly.

"Do you have a favorite pianist?" he asked the men.

"I've read about Horowitz, Chopin, and Liszt, but I don't know enough about them to have a favorite," one of the men answered.

Horowitz and Chopin were faintly familiar. Liszt was new, a name more suited to a flute player. Ashur liked the grinding whisper of it.

He leaned back, his hands still curled about the ends of

the bench. The keys menaced him like eighty-eight sharp teeth ready to snap at his fingers.

He drew a deep breath and balanced himself inwardly for the unreal thing he had to attempt. Now to enlist the uppity woman.

He looked directly at her and said, "I like to put myself in the proper mood before I play. I say to myself, 'Play like the greatest pianist in the world!' It helps my concentration."

He offered his version of a rich, artistic sigh. "You know, I'll tell you something amusing. I've never tried to play like Liszt."

"My, isn't he the modest one!" the woman scoffed. "Listen to him, play like Liszt!"

"Oh, it's just a private game," Ashur said offhandedly. "To tell the truth, Liszt's first name has slipped my mind."

"Franz. Would you like me to spell it for you?" the woman said, nearly choking with derision.

Ashur sighed again, but now genuinely, from relief. He yearned to hug her. She had dropped the name Franz in time— he would become the pianist, not a Liszt who was a shoe-maker or painter or thief. Ten more seconds of his stalling and she'd have dismissed his bluff and marched off victo-riously, beckoning the men to follow. He would have lost the help he needed to escape from the two dark-suits.

His hands moved from the edges of the piano bench and rested limply in his lap.

The Power was in him. It *had* to be in him!

I wish I were Franz Liszt, he thought.

A faraway hum . . . and his wrists lifted gracefully. His

chest rose as if inhaling some stupendous fragrance from the heavens. Then his fingers were rushing across the keys.

He played as no one had played in a hundred years. Ashur Fine—now Franz Liszt, the greatest virtuoso of his day—performed in perfect control of his instrument. Fingers that had worked four or five hours daily at exercises commanded the keys with an exquisite, silvery touch. Mind and hands reached from the past to wrap his audience in sound, the sound of the *Mephisto Waltz.* By comparison, anything played thereafter in the store would blare like a musical Tower of Babel.

Franz-Ashur struck the last note. The piano, the room were still.

Someone clapped. Ashur looked up. The store was crammed with people. Outside the open door, men, women, and children had stopped in the mall to listen. The applause swelled from the single pair of hands to the entire throng of shoppers.

"Bravo!" the slender woman sang, wonder-struck. "Bravo! Bravo!" Ms. Touchy had become Ms. Gushy. "Franz Liszt himself couldn't have done much better!"

"You must have practiced that piece for months and months," a man said in a small, awed voice.

From far in the back someone shouted, "More, more!" Instantly the two words were chanted in rowdy chorus, "More, more!"

"Go on, *please.* Play something else, anything you like," a teenage girl entreated.

"How about Bach's *Concerto for Three Pianos,*" Ashur

37

joked. He rose to his feet, for Franz Liszt was present in him still and had to be dragged from the piano. The virtuoso had accomplished his mission. He had drawn a crowd.

Unforeseeably, the music had cast *too* much charm. The slender woman gripped his elbow. She begged him to stay at the piano when all he wanted to do was use the crowd for his getaway.

He let Liszt take over. Like a robot, Ashur took the woman's hand, bowed with Old World gallantry, and kissed her on the back of her fingertips.

"It is a useful piano, madame," he told her loftily. "Your church will have good service from it."

She had delayed him for only a moment, but the harm was done. The news that he was finished playing spread swiftly. The store emptied as if someone had waved a scatter gun. In the mall, listeners turned back into shoppers. Gone was the crowd he needed to lose the two dark-suits.

He was debating his next move when hunger rescued him. The church committee had decided to buy the piano. As soon as the paperwork was completed, they were all going for a bite to eat in the west end of the shopping center. The woman begged Ashur to join them.

He accepted gratefully, though for a reason she could never guess. She and the three men were his safe conduct from the music shop.

At the restaurant, he couldn't bring himself to order, though he was hungry enough to eat a farm. It was wrong to accept the committee's hospitality when all he wanted to do was run. He glanced at the menu, laid it aside, and excused himself for a moment.

In the men's room he saw what he most desperately needed: a window. As he squirmed through it, he wondered if Franz Liszt had a stout pair of running legs.

He dropped to the ground and discovered Liszt's presence in him had elapsed. His legs were his own, his speed was his own, and together they carried him safely to Aunt Ruth's station wagon.

Ten minutes of driving a curlicue course sufficed. No tailing headlights stuck to his rearview mirror. He had given the dark-suits the slip.

He drove around for another few minutes to be sure. He had enough gas to drive about thirty miles, but he still had no place to spend the night.

He couldn't go home. The dark-suits had been parked on the block when he'd returned from Darlene Morrison's house this afternoon. They'd have his house staked out.

But why? Who were they? What did they want? Ashur needed a night to try to put things together and perhaps become the hunter. He had the Power. . . .

Yet he dared not endanger his friends by asking them for a night's lodging. Dark-suits probably had the low-down on all his acquaintances. Dark-suits seemed to know everything, to have all the answers.

There *was* someone he could ask—Darlene. Hey, the dark-suits couldn't possibly connect her to him. He had never dated her before today.

She opened her front door looking rough-and-tumble in a gray sweat suit and sneakers. The honey-colored hair was tousled boyishly. She had just returned from jogging, she said. If she was surprised to find him on her doorstep, she covered up with a perfect smile.

"I need a place to stay tonight," he said. "I'm in trouble."

She opened the door wider. "Come inside."

"Who is it, Darlene?" a voice called from upstairs.

"A friend, Mother," Darlene responded. To Ashur she said, "You don't look frightened. You look hungry. C'mon into the kitchen."

She lit a front burner on the stove and took ham and three eggs from the refrigerator. While the food cooked, they made light, throwaway conversation. The ham was sizzling before she asked, "Can't your family put you up for the night?"

"I don't have a family," he said. "I've lived with my aunt since I was six. My mother died the year I was born. My father was killed in an airplane crash."

He spoke guardedly, as though afraid his tiny store of memories could trickle out with the words. He recalled his father as a chuckling man who had arms for one purpose only, to lift and cradle him. The memories of his mother stemmed from Aunt Ruth, who was her sister.

Darlene said, "I'm missing something. Why can't you go home? Did you fight with your aunt?"

"My aunt was mugged and knocked to the ground today. She's in Memorial Hospital."

He told her about his mysterious pursuers (omitting his feat at the piano) and got as far as the washroom in the restaurant. By then dark-suit blond and dark-suit bald sounded like escapees from a low-budget comedy, and he himself crazier than a quilt. He gave it up.

"I need a place to stay tonight," he repeated.

Darlene looked at him intently. "I can't put you up in the house, of course," she said at last. "Mother and Dad would throw a tantrum." She smiled. "But I have a place."

When he had finished eating, she led him by the hand to a cabin cruiser moored at the seawall behind the house. "You'll find the key under the dock box," she said. "Put it back when you leave. You can sleep in the saloon on the convertible couch, and no one will be the wiser."

They were out in the moonlight. He ran his arm around her waist, and her nearness suddenly made the shadowed, crystal-hard whiteness of yachts and canals and houses the greenest spot on earth for him. She brushed back strands of hair, freeing her lips. Softly she kissed him good-night and with a murmur hastened across the back lawn toward the house.

He could not fall asleep. He lay in the yacht and grappled with the puzzling dark-suits. They eluded him like vapors.

He called on the Power. I wish I were a dark-suit, he thought.

He waited for the onset of a change, a talent, a novel sensation unfurling through his fingers or shoulders or legs or mind.

He waited, and absolutely nothing happened.

He understood what was wrong. He abandoned the dark-suits. In all probability they had mistaken him for someone else, anyway.

Okay. If he couldn't use the Power in his own behalf, he could use it for Aunt Ruth.

Anger flared in him. Why hadn't the man—what was his

name? Otto Lindt?—why hadn't he helped her against the mugger? Why had he stood by while she was struck and robbed?

Questions unlocked questions. Who was Otto Lindt? Why had he closeted himself in a seedy, downtown hotel to avoid testifying about a collision? He hadn't been in either car. He and a policeman were the only eyewitnesses, Aunt Ruth had said. Had Otto Lindt noticed something about the accident that the policeman had missed? Otto Lindt was as much a mystery as the dark-suits. Who was he?

The dark-suits were beyond the Power, Ashur realized, because he didn't know their names. But Otto Lindt, unlike the dark-suits, had a name. And unquestionably he had seen whoever had mugged Aunt Ruth. For Aunt Ruth, then.

I wish, he thought, I were Otto Lindt.

SIX
THE FORKED BRANCH

ASHUR shuddered as if from a sudden chill. Otto Lindt had come like a strum of the supernatural.

Ashur peered out at the night sky, half prepared to see a monstrous sun soar above the pitch-dark horizon and the moon reel from its orbit.

Outside the cabin window the universe displayed its normal face to earth. The sky sparkled like an endless black cushion to which stars were pinned. The moon remained a bright, steadfast disk in the foreground.

Aside from the hint that he tinkered with the unknown, Otto Lindt was inactive. Ashur grew impatient. He became possessed of a hankering to leave the yacht and examine trees. Without warning, his hands lifted as if jerked by strings. They reached in front of him and briefly clenched an object that wasn't there.

He locked the cabin and replaced the key under the dock box as Darlene had instructed. Walking toward the street, he studied the trees. He disregarded the rubbery fronds of the palms. His eyes hunted among the stiff branches of two Florida oaks and, farther on, the black olives that lined the road.

The oaks and olives had recently been pruned. He passed them by, disappointed.

He had parked Aunt Ruth's station wagon a hundred yards down the block to mislead the dark-suits, should they be out searching. He started for the car, but he was overruled and persuaded in the opposite direction. Otto Lindt yearned for the trash pile on the corner of the Morrisons' property.

The bulk of the trash pile consisted of yard cuttings—branches of trees and bushes, along with some fuzzy, dried-up coconuts. The pile extended about ten feet along the road. Ashur explored it, careful of the spikes that projected from many of the palm fronds.

One after another he hauled free branches from oak or olive trees, rejected them, and heaved them atop the pile. He searched for three or four minutes before digging out an oak branch to his liking.

He went to work with his pocketknife.

He sheared off all but two of the side branches, which then poked out like rabbits' ears. He shortened the stem to eighteen inches. He sawed and whittled for balance, weight, and symmetry, his hands guiding the blade with confident strokes. All the while he hummed "London Bridge."

By and by he folded the blade and replaced the knife in his pocket.

He stared dumbly at Otto Lindt's specialty: a stick with two prongs. It made an oversized but tolerably good frame for a slingshot. So what?

Ashur grimaced with disgust. He was about to chuck away the stick when it did something freakish: It pulsed.

His right hand was holding one of the prongs. As the

pulsing fledged into quivering, he grasped the other prong. The stem leveled out and tugged insistently.

He followed, doddering across the lawn. With every step the tugging and quivering became stronger. He passed the east side of Darlene's house and was pulled to the canal in back. The stick quivered violently.

Ashur braced himself on the top of the concrete seawall. The stick dipped thirstily toward the water, bending him over. He tottered on his toes. The pull had become so urgent that it threatened to yank him into the canal.

He let go. The branch splashed into the water. It floated rigidly, lifelessly, a piece of forked deadwood.

He watched it float on the outgoing tide toward Biscayne Bay. He had saved himself from a soaking, and he understood.

The branch reminded him of Abby Carr, a classmate. In sixth grade she had done a research project on dowsing, a method of finding substances like minerals and treasure under the ground. The tool most commonly used was a forked branch, and the substance most often sought was *water*.

The Power had not missed, after all. Ashur remembered Aunt Ruth's saying that Otto Lindt had found water for farmers out West. He was a dowser!

"Otto Lindt," Ashur whispered, "you were there. Describe the man who mugged my Aunt Ruth."

He heard nothing in the haunting quiet of the night. Otto Lindt was silent.

So there it was. The Power lasted fifteen minutes. Babe Ruth and Franz Liszt had taught him that. Otto Lindt had occupied him for fifteen minutes and had departed.

Communication, Ashur also understood, wasn't two-way.

If Otto Lindt had something to say, he would have said it of his own free will. He was not bound by the Power to answer a question or comply with a request.

Otto Lindt was still a shaded figure. But two clues had thrown sufficient light on him to cast an outline. Clue One, he was a dowser. When the public library opened in the morning, Ashur would be there to follow up Clue Two—Lindt's whereabouts. Until tomorrow, there wasn't a thing to be done except to stay out of sight of the dark-suits.

He curled up in the back of the station wagon rather than spend the night aboard the yacht. He must have been more desperate than he realized to let Darlene put him there. He dreaded to think of the fireworks that would explode if her father was an early riser and spied him sneaking ashore in the morning.

He closed his eyes, intending to grab a catnap. The strains of the nursery jingle "London Bridge" droned through his head again. He began humming and got to the second "falling down" before he sank into exhausted sleep.

A bus with a bad muffler woke him at twenty minutes past seven. He rubbed his sleep-swollen face, stretched, yawned, scrambled into the front seat, and drove off.

If the Gold Star Hotel appeared squalid and groggy at night, by daylight the entire neighborhood looked like a place where small businesses come to die. Ashur approached the hotel cautiously as he searched for Winkie.

Either the dark-suits were sleeping late or the hotel where Aunt Ruth had tried to serve Otto Lindt with a subpoena meant nothing to them. They were nowhere around.

He drove slowly up South Sixth Street. Winkie wasn't trotting on the sidewalk or snooping in the garbage pails. He's probably already home, Ashur thought.

The little dog would find his way, and Mrs. Sonnenberg, the widow who lived across the street, would see to him. Mrs. Sonnenberg baked chocolate chip cookies. She was famous for them. On the occasion of each new batch, Winkie barked unashamedly outside her kitchen window. He invariably received the handout he craved. Winkie would make out just fine in an emergency.

Ashur quit the search for Winkie and pulled into a pancake house. He counted his money in the palm of his hand—a dollar and seven cents. A scavenger hunt under the seats of the station wagon yielded enough additional coins to buy a decent breakfast.

He telephoned Aunt Ruth at the hospital. She was up at X ray, a nurse told him. He left a message that he would call again in two hours.

He dialed Mrs. Sonnenberg. She had already fed Winkie a bowl of cold cereal and a cookie. He lay snoozing under her kitchen table. "Why not?" she said, agreeing to care for him for a few days.

The branch library in Dadesville on 104th Street opened at nine. Ashur used the *New York Times Index* and the microfilm machine. Rather than trust his memory, he photocopied three newspaper articles. The articles provided a slew of facts about London Bridge.

His next stop was the office of the American Automobile Association. A prim, white-haired lady behind the travel desk removed her eyeglasses with both hands and looked at him skeptically. He showed her his membership card.

"I want to go here," he said. He tapped the name Lake Havasu City where it appeared on one of the photocopies. "I can't pronounce it."

She warmed to him at that. "The accent's on the first syllable. When are you planning to leave?"

"Today."

"The Southwest is a frying pan this time of year," she said. "Would you like the northern route? It's a little longer but cooler."

"The southern route," Ashur said emphatically. "I'm in a hurry."

She went to the cubbyholed wall behind her chair and selected maps and TourBooks and a Triptik. She drew a green line over the roads he would take.

"You'll be passing near some sights of interest," she said. "You'll find them described in the TourBooks."

She stacked the TourBooks, maps, and Triptik neatly and fitted them into a clear plastic bag. She slid the bag over to Ashur.

"Have a nice trip, Mr. Fine," she said.

"I'll try," Ashur replied.

The last stop before calling Aunt Ruth was Hurley's Old-Fashioned Ice Cream Shoppe.

Mr. Hurley was bending over a refrigerated glass showcase, squeezing "Happy Birthday" onto an ice cream cake.

"You're late," he said curtly.

Mr. Hurley lived by the rule that a boss ought to ride his help everlastingly. Otherwise they might forget that a life deprived of serving chocolate bonnets and banana splits must come to grief. Yet if a boy looked ill, Mr. Hurley sent him home and paid him for his shift.

"We're low on strawberry. Make a backup tub," he said.

"I can't work today," Ashur stated. "I came to collect my pay."

"You're giving notice?"

"No, I have to leave town for a while. I need the money."

"You should have told me sooner. I have to know *before* you gallop off on a fling. You owe me that so I can—"

"It's not a fling, Mr. Hurley. Something came up suddenly."

Mr. Hurley heaved a sigh. "All right, for you this once," he said. "What is it? Thirty-one hours?"

"Thirty. And nine hours' work painting your house two weeks ago."

Mr. Hurley reached into his trouser pocket for a roll of bills. He peeled off several as though his hands were crippled with pain. He clawed coins from the bins in the cash register. "That correct?"

Ashur counted the money. It was enough for gas and food. "Yes, sir, it's correct."

Somewhere in Mr. Hurley's expression was concern. "You're an honest boy, Ashur," he said. "A hard worker, clean. If you're in trouble, maybe I can help."

"I can handle this myself," Ashur said. "May I use the phone?"

"If you need more than a minute, use the one in back."

Ashur needed more than a minute. He walked to the back, his innards twisting over how to word the news.

Aunt Ruth answered on the first ring. Her voice was peppy and strong.

There was a delay, she said. She could not be discharged until tomorrow, when the battery of tests had been fully evaluated.

"Hospitals," she declared, "have two gears, low for functioning and high for billing, and one must understand and forgive. A third gear, regard for the patient, was stripped long ago."

They chatted about this and that until Aunt Ruth asked what was wrong. "You don't sound like yourself," she said.

Ashur had to come to it. "I'm leaving Dadesville in a few minutes," he managed. "I'm taking a trip."

"May I ask where you're going?"

The question was typical of her: low-keyed, self-controlled. She didn't remind him that he lacked her permission to leave Dadesville. She didn't trade on her health to tie him to her.

"I'm driving to Lake Havasu City in Arizona," he said. "I'm sure that's where Otto Lindt is. If things work out, I should be back in two weeks."

There was silence on the other end of the line.

Ashur got on with it nervously. He asked if he might borrow the station wagon, which was newer and more reliable than his truck. He avoided mention of the dark-suits, who might be watching for him at home because the truck was there. Aunt Ruth mustn't get involved.

"Promise me you'll stay with Cousin Anne while I'm gone," he begged. "You shouldn't be alone right after the hospital."

"You're not telling me everything," she accused.

He answered with the bare truth. "I'm going after the man who mugged you."

Aunt Ruth uttered a little gasp. "That is a police matter. I've already been given a case number, and now it's out of our hands. I only lost a few dollars."

"You were *hit*," Ashur protested, almost letting the anger in him erupt. "You were knocked to the ground."

"I'm all right now, darling," Aunt Ruth said. "I'll be discharged tomorrow."

Ashur couldn't explain it to her. He wasn't sure he could explain it to himself. Outrage and an inner, screaming call for justice seized hold of him. "I'm going to Arizona," he said evenly. "It's something I have to do."

They spoke for ten minutes more. Ashur parried all objections. He yearned to lay her fears to rest by confiding in her, but he didn't dare. He didn't dare tell anyone about the Power till he knew its wiles and had mastered them.

"I've got money," he said. "Mr. Hurley paid me. If I need more, I can do odd jobs along the way."

She consented in a voice heavy with anxiety. She had reared him to be self-reliant, after all.

"I'll be at Anne's until you come back," she promised. "And . . . Ashur . . ."

"Yes?"

"God bless you and keep you, child."

"God bless you," he whispered.

He hung up and dialed again. A Sergeant Nevers took his description of dark-suit blond and dark-suit bald. "A patrol will check your house for a couple of days," the sergeant said.

51

The call to the Florida Zoo was relayed from desk to desk before he reached a Ms. Kirby-Chaney, head of public relations. She could not, or would not, be specific. The old elephant who had killed the hippos had been chained in the elephant barn since the tragedy.

"Will he stay at the zoo?" Ashur inquired.

"What will be done with him is undecided at this point," she stated, as if reciting a press release.

Ashur thanked her and walked to the station wagon, musing on what might befall anyone who attempted to destroy Methuselah. Could the ancient beast be slain, or was he immortal?

The inside of the station wagon was furnace-hot. Ashur cranked down the front windows. He unfolded the large road map, "Eastern States South," and laid it on the passenger seat. He put the Triptik on top of it and leafed to the first map. The green line traced the early stages of his route: Interstate 95 to Florida's Turnpike.

He turned the ignition key. The engine sounded and shot a tremor through the car. He coasted over a speed bump and drove north on Route 1 toward Interstate 95.

Although he had never been out of Florida, he was setting off across the country to find a man named Otto Lindt. Ashur was sure Lindt could lead him to the person who had hurt Aunt Ruth.

He was young and inexperienced and seemingly defenseless, but he had protection against whatever dangers crouched in Arizona. For he was not making the trip alone.

He had a companion, the Power.

SEVEN
ON THE ROAD

BY nightfall Ashur had completed the long northward drive through the sweltering center of Florida and was heading west across the panhandle to Alabama.

Through the rearview mirror, he watched for headlights that lingered too long. Cars came and went, each pursuing its own course, and he did not see any of them twice.

The sky became a deepening smudge of clouds. A mile after the Tallahassee exit, a light rain started to fall. Two exits farther, the storm broke in a drumming downpour.

Ashur slackened his speed. He maintained thirty-five miles an hour until the storm, moving in the opposite direction, waned. Five minutes later he slowed again. Blinkers flashed under an overpass.

His headlights shone on a black sedan with its hood opened in distress. A man was bending over the engine. A woman stood beside him. When she saw Ashur slow down, she jumped forward and waved to him pleadingly.

Ashur glanced at the man and woman with sharpened eye and awakened pulse. They must have been miles ahead of him when trouble struck. He did not remember seeing a black car. . . .

Nobody'll stop on a night like this, he thought.

Despite a wee voice of warning, he had to do what was right. He braked onto the shoulder of the highway, shifted into reverse, and backed under the sheltering arch of the overpass.

His hand lingered on the door handle. The hour was late and traffic was sparse. He remembered in a vague and generalized way stories of motorists who stopped to lend assistance by the side of the road. Not infrequently they were beaten and robbed in return for their kindness.

Common sense dictated that he protect himself. The Power. . . . If he called upon the Power, the know-how to subdue an armed foe would be his.

Fine and dandy, except that his knowledge of martial artists amounted to zero. He floundered after a name. Nothing came to mind but the covers of karate magazines in convenience stores. As his thoughts roamed farther and farther afield, a picture crossed his memory. It was a photograph he had seen somewhere of a dark, slope-shouldered man with a stony face and lightning in his arms—Joe Louis!

I wish I were Joe Louis, he thought.

He stepped from the station wagon and with straight-legged, shuffling steps walked to the black car. Invisible inside him was a bodyguard beyond comparison, the greatest heavyweight boxing champion in the history of the ring, Joe Louis.

"What seems to be the trouble?" Ashur asked.

The man straightened and slanted his flashlight in

Ashur's direction. "Thanks for stopping, young man. I'm not much of a mechanic—"

"It just quit," the woman broke in impatiently. *"Pfft!"*

"Is it the first time something like this has happened?" Ashur asked.

"Can't say. We rented the bloody car this morning in Miami," the man answered. He was about thirty and so wondrously average-looking as to qualify for a career as a movie extra.

The woman was singular. A tall, large-limbed blonde with thick hands and broad shoulders, she was for all her size shapely and handsome, a belle of the bench press.

"We're supposed to be in Baton Rouge before morning," she said, pouting. "One minute this Detroit crate was running like a top, the next—*zap, pfft!*"

"Sounds like the alternator," Ashur said. He shuffled to the engine.

"That part of the electrical system?" the man said. "I thought it had something to do with the electrical system."

"If you knew so much, how come you didn't repair it?" the woman sneered. She had moved so that the car was between her and the road. Slyly her eyes darted up and down the highway in a series of quick, sentrylike glances.

Ashur kept his head free of the opened hood. He walked slowly around the engine.

"Here's your problem," he said. "The coil wire vibrated loose." He plugged it in. "You'll start up now."

"Praised be," the big woman said. "It's getting on to morning."

"I can't figure how it could have fallen all the way off," Ashur remarked.

"What's the difference?" the man said. "You found the trouble, and orchids to you. I figured the rain had wet the wires, and we'd be marooned here till the sun came up and dried them out."

His voice dwindled after the mention of wet wires, as if he had realized his slip but couldn't stop himself without emphasizing it.

The slip rang in Ashur's ears. Studiously he kept his gaze from the dry windshield of the black car and the shining front fenders and bumper.

The big woman snarled, "Your fat mouth is going to hang us someday, Hal, do you know that?"

Hal flinched as though stung. He shut up and looked away, his face stiff with humiliation. The big woman obviously had put him through an obedience class.

"Get on with it," she ordered.

Hal nodded. "Okay, behind the car, young fella," he said. His back, turned to the highway, shielded the pistol in his hand.

Ashur shuffled into the space between the black car and the supporting wall of the overpass.

The big woman opened the rear door. "Be a dove, love," she cooed, "and come peacefully."

"Do as she says, fella," Hal advised, leering with triumph. "Make her sweat, and she'll have you wishing I'd plugged you."

He wagged the pistol in the direction of the open door. Ashur saw the rapid back-and-forth motions as if they were gloved fists feinting blows. Uncannily, he was able to separate each fraction of movement as though timing a punch through the spaces.

As the barrel of the pistol swung past him in one of its rapid oscillations, he executed a tiny, vital repositioning that squared him to Hal. Then he took a small step to his right and exploded a right hand to the gunman's temple. Before the pistol landed on the ground, the left fist shot out in a short, staving hook.

Hal's cheek rippled like rubber around the impact. He sagged and then, halfway down, lunged forward as if pitching off a chair.

Ashur, who now was the most deadly finisher ever— the Brown Bomber whose six-inch punches few professionals survived—threw the right again in an uppercut and caught the falling Hal in the torso, crunching the ribs over his heart.

Swiftly he kicked the pistol under the black car.

"You're good," the woman said. Her eyes gleamed. "You cleaned up the second string. Now let's see how you fare against the varsity."

"Look after the second string," Ashur countered tartly. "Buy him a hospital. I'm leaving."

"Don't turn your back on me," the woman warned, "or I'll tear your spine off."

She had left the rear door of the car open, and by the dome light he saw her hands chopping the air.

"I don't have unhealthy vices," she purred. "I don't drink and I don't smoke cigars, but once a week I need a fix. So I go to the gym and slam some pretty-boy wrestler."

"Men don't fight women," Ashur said, speaking for himself and Joe Louis.

"Then allow me," she said icily, "to raise your consciousness."

She flashed a wicked smile and without another word closed with him.

The battle was fierce, one-sided. She attacked and Ashur defended. She circled, and he pivoted to keep her in front of him. She struck at him with strong, terrible blows; he blunted them with his arms or deflected them harmlessly into the air. Her kicks were more successful, and she punished his torso and legs before he learned to twist aside and block with his forearms.

She continued hurting him, nevertheless. She was trouncing the heavyweight champion with her strength and skill and his attitude. Joe Louis had sprung from another generation, one that held gallantry to be a virtue. No self-respecting man would dream of striking a woman.

She attacked silently, mercilessly, exultantly. The only sounds were the hard whack and clap of blows and her hoarse breathing. Ashur's arms and shoulders ached from her edge-of-the-hand karate chops, his legs and body sobbed from her Amazonian kicks. Despite the punishment, he did not strike at her.

But eventually there came a point at which Ashur decided he had suffered quite enough. He asserted himself.

"Forgive me," he uttered out loud to Joe Louis and to his own dear, old-fashioned beliefs.

He fought with bruised, leaden arms—without the savage speed of the heavyweight champion. He swung and kicked and grappled according to the rules of survival.

She had been unable to put him away in the freshness of her strength and stamina. Now, wearing down, she was unable to cope with his wild tactics. Gradually she lost both heart and technique.

She panted, and as she stumbled into him, a fist met her full on the jaw. Her legs contracted sideways in a giant, frog-like twitch, and she landed on her bottom. She swayed upright, arms dangling uselessly.

In the frenzy of self-preservation, he hit her again. She sprawled on her back, screamed once faintly, and passed out.

Headlights approached on his side of the highway, pinpricks glittering in the distant darkness. Ashur wiped his face and winced at the blood on the handkerchief. Hal was still out cold from Joe Louis's first punch. Ashur flopped him behind the steering wheel of the black car.

The big woman was coming around. Too weak and beaten to resist, she allowed Ashur to drag and lift and shove her into the seat beside Hal. While partly cradled in Ashur's arms, she fixed him with a glazed and haunted stare. Her lips struggled feebly. He tilted his head to hear. In a low, husky whisper, she cursed him and all his forebears.

Ashur had retrieved the pistol and was pocketing it when the headlights stopped, revealing a white panel truck. "Everything all right?" the driver called.

"We're taking a break," Ashur said. "My friends needed to catch forty winks."

"Don't nap here," the driver said, appalled. "Wake 'em up. Get off in two exits. You'll see three motels all in a clump."

"We'll do that," Ashur said. "Much obliged, mister."

The driver smiled and shook his head in disbelief. "This is no place to fall asleep," he said, and tossed a farewell salute.

As the taillights of the truck receded, Ashur hurled the pistol as far as he could into the trees bordering the highway. He picked up the flashlight and shone it on the engine of the black car. He ripped out every wire he saw and slammed the hood shut.

"What'd you do in there?" the woman demanded shrilly.

"I located your trouble," Ashur said. "Your wires aren't wet. They're disconnected."

"You can't leave us stranded out here, you miserable kid!" the woman shrieked. The female fighting machine had sputtered into a lump of hysterical rantings. "It's getting to be some country when creeps like you run around beating up women!"

She was still shrieking as he started up the station wagon. He got back on the highway without bothering to wave good-bye.

EIGHT
THE ANDERSON DIAMOND

LITTLE by little, Ashur was becoming acquainted with the Power. The experience at the overpass confirmed something that he already suspected. And it introduced him to something frightening.

The visits of Babe Ruth, Franz Liszt, and Otto Lindt had suggested that the Power lasted for roughly fifteen minutes. Joe Louis proved it. His departure had been impossible to miss. All at once Ashur had stopped hurting.

The aches pounded into him by the blonde Amazon had vanished. Simultaneously, the torn skin and bruises about his knuckles had healed without a scar. He stroked his face exploringly. The cuts were gone.

The healing alarmed him. One explanation only was possible. When Joe Louis departed, he took with him all the physical signs of his visit.

Suppose, Ashur thought, he had not knocked out Hal and beaten the big blonde to the ground. Suppose he had been killed by Hal's pistol. After Joe Louis had departed from him, might he have returned to life as whole and healthy as before, without a trace of a bullet wound?

The concept hounded him as he drove toward Arizona ahead of the rising sun. It hinted that while another personality dwelt in him, he was deathless.

Surely Methuselah had not meant for him to have such an unholy faculty. Could the Power be growing in him in spite of Methuselah's intention to limit it? Had the elephant lost control when the hippos raised such a ruckus of protest?

Ashur rubbed his eyes. He needed sleep. Exhaustion was getting to him. His thoughts wandered back to Hal and the big blonde. They hadn't taken his money. They had tried to force him into their car. Why? If they weren't thieves, who were they? What were they really after?

He turned on the radio. A rasping rock group brought his mind to a raw and jagged wakefulness.

He drove on. He crossed the southern tip of Mississippi and entered Louisiana. At Theodore he turned south off Interstate 10 and followed Route 90 along the Gulf of Mexico. If the dark-suits still were after him, they would not look for him on a secondary road.

He passed the kind of folksy, slumbering towns that America is built on. He had to sleep soon. Half an hour into Louisiana, he saw a sign announcing West Gulfport. According to his Triptik, West Gulfport was a popular resort. He scouted its main streets before selecting the hotel with the most crowded parking lot.

He combed his hair and straightened his shirt. In the large, cheaply modernized lobby, he bought a newspaper from a vending machine. He carried it to an overstuffed love seat and opened it casually, as if waiting to meet someone.

He read the headlines and fell fast asleep.

When he awoke, the lobby had come alive with the low, incessant chorus of scattered conversations. At the far end, a line of hotel guests and townies stood waiting to get into the coffee shop.

He felt rested and glanced at his watch. He had slept past midday.

Suddenly he became aware of another person on the love seat with him.

"Sleep well?"

He saw a woman in her forties with a chic, professional look. She stared at his hands.

He smiled self-consciously and fidgeted with the newspaper on his lap. "I never made it to the registration desk last night," he said, in case she was a house detective.

"You don't mind my speaking to you, do you?" she asked. "You have such beautiful hands."

Ashur tightened. He waited without knowing for what.

"Marvelous hands," the woman went on with the enthusiasm of a museum guide. "I've been looking at them for half an hour and wondering."

"I never thought much about them," Ashur said uncomfortably.

"Oh, you should, young man." The woman stirred as if preparing to rise. "Hands like yours belong to a pianist or a prizefighter. Now which, I've been asking myself, is it?"

"Neither," Ashur said. "I'm a high-school student."

She did up her lips in a taunting smile. Ashur seized the moment to excuse himself. He sprang from the love seat and

63

went to the lobby entrance. The station wagon was a hundred feet from the door. His hand slid into his pocket and closed about the ignition key.

"Don't even think about it," the woman said. She had come up beside him. "Take a good look."

Parked right beyond the station wagon was a familiar car. He didn't have to see more than the color of the trunk lid. It was the gray sedan that had trailed him to the hospital and shopping center in Dadesville. The dark-suits had overtaken him.

Dark-suit bald appeared from nowhere. He looked tired and his once flawlessly pressed suit suffered from twenty-four-hour wrinkles. "Ready, Boola?" he said.

"Yes, let's go," the woman said.

"Hey, what's this all about?" Ashur demanded.

"You," Boola said. "Come with us. We'll give you a run-down later."

"You're making a mistake," Ashur said, and took a stab at humor. "People are always saying I look like somebody else."

"Funny boy," Boola said.

Dark-suit bald shoved his right hand furtively inside his jacket and held the pose melodramatically. He made a sinister tapping motion, as if to show that he wasn't relieving heartburn.

"A thirty-eight equipped with a silencer sounds about as loud as a kid's air gun," he warned Ashur in a barely audible voice. "It might even be mistaken for a wine bottle being opened in a restaurant."

Ashur had heard silencers muffle gunshots in the movies.

They sounded very little like a BB gun and entirely unlike a cork popping. But he conceded the point without argument. He smiled, shrugged, and flashed his palms.

"Let's go," Boola said again with a reinforcing prod.

"I have to go to the bathroom first," Ashur announced.

Boola hesitated before agreeing to it. "Go with him," she ordered curtly.

Ashur walked across the lobby with dark-suit bald on his heels. The door to the men's room opened onto a short, poorly lighted corridor. Along one wall was a maroon door, and beyond it were a vending machine for cigarettes and another for toiletries. Half hidden on the wall between the machines was a telephone. Pushing open the maroon door, Ashur hoped that he was blocking dark-suit bald's view of the corridor— and the telephone.

He entered the tiled lavatory. It was empty and without windows. A dead end.

"You ran out of luck," dark-suit bald gloated.

Ashur marched into a stall and locked the door.

"Five minutes," dark-suit bald said.

"Leave me in peace or I'll be in here until housecleaning arrives," Ashur rejoined, the words sounding without a trace of the fear scraping his throat. "Then you'll hear screaming like you've never heard before. I'll scream I'm stuck. It'll take the fire rescue squad to free me."

"I'll wait for you by the sinks," dark-suit bald said gruffly.

"You'll get yourself arrested for loitering before I come out," Ashur retorted. "Wait in the lobby, and I'll be out in ten minutes."

"Boola won't allow more than five," dark-suit bald

growled. "Be out in five or you're out forever. I'll put so many holes in that door it'll look like a high rise for mice."

"Ten minutes," Ashur insisted, and wasted one of them listening while dark-suit bald made up his mind, muttered grudging approval, and stamped out.

Ashur dropped a coin into the pay telephone in the corridor. The operator gave him the number of the police department. He stretched a handkerchief over the mouthpiece to disguise his voice. He told an officer that he'd seen a puppy locked in a station wagon with the windows up. The officer was properly angered. Ashur gave her the license plate number, and she promised to send a unit over to the hotel directly.

Having done what he could, Ashur returned to the stall and read his newspaper.

Below the fold on the first page was a boxed story with the headline: TED WILSON TAKES SECRET TO GRAVE.

Ashur skimmed the story.

> Ted Wilson died in prison of a heart attack yesterday at the age of 71, three months before his parole hearing. Wilson, convicted of the theft of the famed Anderson diamond seven years ago, never revealed the hiding place of the gem. He was employed for 18 years at the old H. M. Peters Company plant in West Gulfport, which is scheduled to be demolished to make room for a drive-in bank.

The account tantalized. Why? Was it the similarity between himself and Ted Wilson? Wilson had been imprisoned for theft. Trapped in a hotel rest room, Ashur, too, was a prisoner, though without knowing why.

When the police arrived, they might free him from Boola

66

and the dark-suits. Or they might complicate matters. If he could eliminate the risk. If he had some other advantage . . .

Ashur reread the newspaper story. Was there something else?

His gaze steadied on the one line: "never revealed the hiding place of the gem."

I wish I were Ted Wilson, he thought.

His lips puckered and his cheeks puffed out, but no sound issued forth. Whatever his specialty, Ted Wilson wasn't a whistler. Perhaps the old H. M. Peters Company had manufactured musical instruments, and Ted Wilson had tested clarinets, French horns, and trumpets.

Ashur viewed his puffed cheeks in the mirror above the sinks. He looked as if he'd swallowed a pair of water wings.

He expelled the air and, yielding to an impulse, bent over. From this gawky position, hands on knees and neck craning, he had a charming view of the scum under the sinks and the tarnished pipes. His hand, as if gifted with a mind of its own, went to the curved trap in a leaky drainpipe.

The message seemed clear. Ted Wilson hadn't tested wind instruments for the H. M. Peters Company. He probably had worked as a handyman or janitor.

Thanks for your help, Ted Wilson, and rest in peace, Ashur thought, ideas swirling in his head.

With a little luck, Boola and the dark-suits could be made to look as if they were in town to swipe the stolen Anderson diamond from a pipe in an H. M. Peters Company washroom! All Ashur had to do was drop a hint into the proper ear. By the time the West Gulfport police sorted things out, he would be in Arizona.

A minute was left of the ten he had bullied from dark-suit bald. Ashur took a deep breath and walked into the lobby.

Dark-suit bald brushed against him before he'd gone three feet. Boola brushed him from the other side. She reached behind his back and clasped hands with dark-suit bald.

"You mustn't drink so early in the day, darling," Boola reproved Ashur gaily, like a mother covering up her humiliation.

The pressure of their arms against his back jogged Ashur's legs into a lurching, drunken gait. And the pressure of the gun in his ribs jogged his mind: A drunk person and a wounded person walk with a stagger. He chose the blood-less imitation of a drunk over resistance.

As the three of them passed from the hotel, dark-suit blond emerged from the gray sedan. He was opening the doors when the West Gulfport police car appeared.

The policemen—Ashur was glad to see two—came over to the station wagon, taking the scene in slowly as they approached. They had the stocky builds and budding paunches of former high-school linebackers thriving in their brown uniforms.

"That's my car," Ashur volunteered. "Is there something wrong?"

"Let's find out," one of the officers said. "Mind opening her up?"

Ashur unlocked the station wagon and opened the four doors. The officer poked his head inside, peered around, and pulled back.

"False alarm, Earl," he said irritably to the other policeman.

"Mind telling me what this is all about?" Ashur asked.

"Got a tip about a puppy being locked in this car with the windows up," the policeman said. His mouth twisted coarsely. "Some smart aleck—"

"You got it, Luther. I'll bet it was that Beattie kid again," Earl said.

"I don't have a dog with me," Ashur said innocently.

"Where you headin', young fella?" Earl demanded.

"El Paso," Ashur replied, with just the mildest hesitation.

Earl gestured toward the dark-suits and Boola, who had retreated a few paces and were standing by the gray car. "You all together?"

"No, we just struck up a conversation in the lobby," Boola said.

"We ate lunch at nearby tables," Ashur said, and felt the flick of Boola's baleful glance.

"Well, it's all been a mistake, folks," Luther admitted. "Sorry."

"Drive safely and have a nice day," Earl added.

Ashur was in the station wagon with the doors locked and the engine running as the policemen reached their patrol car. He backed alongside them and leaned out the window.

"Pardon me, officers," he said. "Is there a rock quarry in West Gulfport?"

"Never heard of one," Earl answered.

"Oh. Well, how about a musical instrument factory?"

"Not one of those, either."

Ashur made his face long with disappointment while he fumbled for the target. *Puffed cheeks.* . . . "How about a glass factory, a place where men blow glass?"

Earl unwrapped a stick of gum and consulted Luther.

"They blew glass in the old H. M. Peters plant on Michigan Road," Luther said. "It's no tourist attraction, unless you freak out on old bricks and broken windows. Been empty going on six years."

"I was sort of hoping for something more romantic. I don't turn on to old buildings or old plumbing," Ashur said. He spoke slowly, pronouncing each word clearly. "But those people getting into the gray sedan are nuts about rocks. I overheard them at lunch."

"That so?" Earl commented incuriously.

"Yeah, they were talking about going out to some old place to look for a rock," Ashur went on. "Imagine getting all worked up over rocks! They jabbered a lot about two men named Anderson and Wilson, especially Wilson. Seems he was a glass blower who dropped a rock down a sink in the men's room. Got jailed for it or something."

"Couldn't happen," Earl muttered indifferently. "No such law."

Ashur's hopes sank. He had laid it all out. He had planted the seed, but seemingly into barren heads. Earl sat there and pushed the stick of gum into his mouth.

"Take care, y'hear?" Ashur called, and drove to the hotel exit arrow. Traffic on the avenue was moderate, and he might have snaked in at any time. Instead he turned in his seat and observed the police car.

Wasn't "rock" a nationally accepted slang word for a precious stone, like the stolen Anderson diamond? How could *both* policemen have missed the connection with Ted Wilson? Surely they'd seen the newspaper story. . . .

Dark-suit blond had backed the gray car out of the parking space when a horn sounded for him to stop. Earl stood by the police car and unsnapped his holster. Glowering sullenly, Luther strode to the gray car.

It had taken them exasperatingly long to turn over and over in their minds what Ashur had said. But they had labored to the right conclusion.

Ashur gunned the station wagon away from the hotel.

He felt almost guilty about leaving Boola and the dark-suits to unsnarl themselves from the law. They'd be delayed at least until the washrooms in the old H. M. Peters Company plant had been searched. If, in fact, Ted Wilson had hidden the stolen Anderson diamond in a trap under a sink, all the better. Boola and the dark-suits would be tied up in West Gulfport for a good while.

Either way, Ashur had gained precious hours. Soon he'd be clear of Louisiana and in Texas.

NINE
THE ANIMAL HOSPITAL

HE traveled the mammoth breadth of Texas—from the flat, low prairies of the southeast to the high plains of the west.

Once more he was pushing too hard, overworking the engine and himself. He had been driving so far and so long that he had almost forgotten how it was to run and jump.

He stopped in the outskirts of El Paso and put up at a motor court that was perfect, being handy and cheap. It offered eight little wood cabins. The cabin assigned to him smelled of bug spray and the accumulated odor of twenty thousand thrifty yesterdays.

He scarcely recalled stretching out. When he awoke, he was lying fully clothed on top of the musty bedding. He had slept soundly for seven hours. He felt strengthened, but grubby and unwashed.

He found an Army & Navy Store. He bought two shirts, two pairs of socks, a three-pack of shorts, toothbrush and toothpaste. Returning to the cabin, he cleaned up, changed clothing, and got back on Interstate 10.

"Otto Lindt, I'm coming," he breathed.

From El Paso he drove the highway across the bottom

of New Mexico and into Arizona. His destination, Lake Havasu City, lay to the west, up against the California border.

By now he was flushed with confidence. He had outwitted the dark-suits and the woman Boola at West Gulfport. No vehicle had tailed him through Nevada and Texas. No driver in distress, pretended or genuine, had waved to him for help.

The strains of "London Bridge" rollicked through his head.

He left the highway at nightfall rather than drive the last one hundred and fifty miles in darkness. Whatever awaited him was best met by an alert and rested mind.

In Yuma Bend he stopped for a tuna fish sandwich at a cafeteria on the main street. Afterward he parked in front of the police headquarters. He locked the doors of the station wagon and lay down in the cargo space.

Before his joints had come together, he was behind the wheel again as dawn sprayed the vast, dulling emptiness of Arizona with light and teeming heat.

The car sped onward and onward. A few miles past Parker Junction he saw the first sign to Lake Havasu City. His heart skipped and leaped with joy. The last leg, the home stretch, the run for Otto Lindt!

Lake Havasu City looked exactly as he had expected from his research in the Dadesville library: a community planted in the middle of the desert by a bold, hunch-playing million-aire land developer. The "chicken coop," as Ashur thought of it, was the selling point. It drew hordes of tourists, many of whom bought lots or houses or condominiums and settled in the mushrooming city.

"If you wish to catch a fox," Aunt Ruth had counseled,

"don't bother to don a red coat and a derby hat and ride to the hounds. Find some shade and watch the chicken coop."

Without having to ask directions, Ashur found his "chicken coop": a thousand-foot span of five graceful stone arches with a man-made channel flowing underneath—London Bridge!

Otto Lindt, his fox, was here. Ashur was convinced of it. The song "London Bridge" had possessed his mind when Otto Lindt entered him at Darlene Morrison's house. Oh, yes, Otto Lindt was in Lake Havasu City, all right, in a place from which he had a view of the bridge.

To find him, to pinpoint his window, Ashur had to look within himself.

He cleared his mind and tried to relax. I wish I were Otto Lindt, he thought.

When, in the cabin of the Morrisons' yacht, he had made the same wish, Otto Lindt had alighted in him immediately. Now, although he thought the name with the urgency of an obsession, the Power remained inactive.

The minutes slipped away. Two . . . three . . .

Ashur sat helplessly, his legs thrust limply against the floorboard of the car.

Four minutes . . . five . . .

He still sat in the same position, but his legs had gone rigid, and he closed his eyes as he grew more and more tense and alarmed. With dogged desperation, he cried out, "Do you hear? *I wish I were Otto Lindt!*"

It was no use. Even if he were to repeat the wish a hundred times, Otto Lindt would not respond.

Failure added an unwelcome fact to Ashur's knowledge

of the Power. Once summoned, a visitor did a fifteen-minute shift and departed forever. Otto Lindt was never to be recalled.

Ashur resigned himself. He had expected Otto Lindt somehow to indicate where he was in Lake Havasu City.

It was not to be so easy.

Otto Lindt had witnessed the attack on Aunt Ruth. Ashur intended to find him, if not with the magic of the Power, then with the power of imagination and the sweat of persistence.

Near one end of London Bridge stood an "English" village, a group of shops built in Tudor style. There, at the London Bridge gift shop, Ashur scanned the telephone book. Otto Lindt was not listed.

There had to be some name he could summon. . . .

He tried "Hal," the gunman whom Joe Louis had kayoed under the overpass. He tried "Boola," the woman who had tried to kidnap him in West Gulfport. He tried "dark-suit bald" and "dark-suit blond" again.

To each of these names the Power remained steadfastly unheeding and silent, as Ashur knew it must. To summon the Power he had to think *both* names and not just a first name or last name, a nickname such as Boola, or a name he had made up, such as dark-suit blond or dark-suit bald.

He primed his imagination and aimed it inward.

Hidden in some crevice of his subconscious mind, in the gray, wet wilderness of cells and fluids, was the clue to Otto Lindt's whereabouts. Ashur strained for it. He pictured his brain being scrambled over by tiny detective-workmen. They did his bidding: They sloshed through the fluids and rooted under membranes and nerve cells with their tiny picks and shovels.

Eventually they located the clue. With cries of triumph they goaded it from its lair and sent it wriggling up into Ashur's conscious mind. He pounced before it escaped.

Boola. . . .

At first he did not understand. Then his lips quivered and shaped the rowdy, joyful tune—the Yale "Boola Boola" song! Northeast High School's marching band had played it last year, and he had read about it in one of the Yale University catalogs in his bedroom. How had he overlooked anything so odd and obvious as her nickname!

He reopened the telephone book and flipped the pages to "Yale."

Her listing stood out as if printed in raised letters. He stared dumbfounded, hardly able to absorb his good fortune. There it was, between "Yaeger, John C." and "Yardley, Lamar"—"Yale, Beulah, D.V.M."

The address was a one-story brown building on Delano Street. In front stood a green sign with yellow lettering on two lines: YALE ANIMAL CLINIC above, and below, in smaller letters, *Beulah Yale, Doctor of Veterinary Medicine.*

Ashur circled the block. Two windows in the side of the brown building faced London Bridge. A discovery almost as important was the Laundromat. Situated across the street from the animal hospital, it made an ideal observation post.

He parked and rolled his soiled clothes into a ball. To increase the bulk to a size worthy of laundering, he added the new shirt, socks, and underwear he had bought in El Paso.

The Laundromat had two customers. Ashur had his choice of washing machines and selected one near the door. While the fill cycle ran, he telephoned the animal hospital.

The metallic voice of a recorded message clicked on. "The hospital will be closed until September first, while Dr. Yale is on vacation. If you will please leave your message, name, and number at the sound of the tone, she will return your call when the hospital reopens."

Ashur hung up.

He watched the hospital until the washing machine had completed the spin cycle and shut off. No one had entered or left the brown building.

To justify staying in the Laundromat, he ran his clothes a second time. The attendant, a young woman of about eighteen or nineteen, came over to him.

"Are you having a problem?" she asked politely.

"No, my clothes were really dirty," Ashur said sheepishly. "They needed a second washing."

"Why don't you try a bleach?" she suggested. She was a gaunt, homely young woman with straggly hair. Her skin was parched, as if it had been baked dry by the constant, whirling heat of the machines around her.

Ashur bought a packet of powdered bleach. He had washed his skimpy load again and was watching it tumble in the drier when a brown van stopped before the animal hospital. The driver got out carrying a cardboard tray filled with three or four white paper bags. Napkins and straws protruded from one of the bags.

The man knocked on the animal hospital door, quick raps with the knuckle of his arched forefinger. Presently the door opened, and the man disappeared inside.

Ashur wondered about what he had seen as he scooped his clothes from the drier and began folding them. He happened to look up and caught the young woman watching him. Instantly her eyes moved away like a startled rabbit's, and her pale face filled with color.

How often had he looked away with the same timorous, rabbity quickness when Darlene Morrison had caught him staring at her in class. . . .

He laid his clothes on the front counter. "My dog, Winkie, has a case of fleas," he said. "I ought to take him to a vet. Do you know anything about Dr. Yale across the street?"

"She's good," the young woman said, "but expensive. I took my Rhett to her for shots last year."

"Maybe I'll ask about her fee first," Ashur said jokingly.

The woman's pale, homely face relaxed, as though she were pleased that he had opened conversation. She seemed about to switch the subject, but then changed her mind or lost her courage. "Dr. Yale is on vacation," she said. "The hospital is closed."

"I don't think so," Ashur said. "A man went into the building while I was drying my clothes. Maybe some other vet is treating the animals. Doctors cover for one another. Vets probably do the same."

"You're correct," the young woman said. "The place isn't *closed* closed. At least twice a day someone brings food from a take-out place in town."

"Maybe Dr. Yale is boarding a mutt with a fancy appetite," Ashur said.

The young woman shook her head. "I haven't heard a dog bark in three days."

Three days. . . . There was a connection somewhere,

78

Ashur thought. Three days ago he had begun the drive from Florida to Arizona.

Suddenly a part of him became aware of danger. He was standing too near the front of the Laundromat. He could be seen from the animal hospital.

Hurriedly he picked up his small stack of washed clothes. "Nice talking to you, miss," he said.

"I enjoyed it, too," she replied with a little smile.

He drove to the English village. Looking across the water, he saw the back of the animal hospital. If he could not see the faces of whoever entered and departed, neither could he be seen spying.

He browsed the village shops, had a hamburger and cream soda, and waited for the darkness to reveal what he wished to know. From a corner videotape store, he watched the sun set and night pour forth its mysteries.

House by house, the lights of Lake Havasu City went on, until at last it happened. Two windows and then a third lit up in the animal hospital, the building that was supposed to be closed.

It was time to act.

TEN
THE PRISONER

HE had two errands to do before he put his courage to the test.

At an all-night convenience store, he bought a can of tuna fish. Then, for an hour, he scoured the dark back alleys of Lake Havasu City. Behind Chin's Chinese Restaurant, the search ended. He heard a meow.

A pair of cats foraged in the garbage pails, their watchful yellow eyes ashine with suspicion. At the scrunch of Ashur's footsteps, they scampered out of sight.

Ashur opened the can of tuna fish by the tab. He underhanded a mushy scrap to the edge of the pails.

The cats padded into the open. They sniffed tentatively and licked up the splattering of fish.

Ashur held out the can. The cats refused to come closer, but neither did they leap away. He put the can on the ground and moved back one step.

Presently the larger cat padded forward with cautious dignity, regal as a hobo warlord. Its companion, a runt that looked like a burnt shoe brush with tufts of fur pasted on, followed timidly.

Ashur let the runt gobble a mouthful before grasping it gently by the neck. "Don't be afraid," he murmured.

At once the hideous little creature became trustful and content. When Ashur released it in the cargo space of the station wagon, it jumped eagerly into the front seat to be with him.

Ashur stroked the loose hide, rippling it over the bumpy, meatless ribs. The yellow eyes closed contentedly, making him wonder. When the Power was new, both Winkie and the goldfish had felt its presence in him instantly. They had been frightened. Unlike them, this ugly runt nestling against him was relaxed and accepting. . . .

Something he should have noticed before was happening. The Power was more than just growing in him. It was becoming a normal part of him, as normal as his friendship with animals. More, it was strengthening his tie to animals.

Was it possible? Could he now control animals? Was the little cat—indeed, were all the other animals of the earth—at his beck and call?

He stared at the fur-coated sack of bones flopped out beside him on the seat of the car.

Roll over, he thought.

The cat meowed obediently, squirmed onto its side, and lay with legs outstretched.

Roll back.

The cat rolled back.

Ashur's lips pursed. He drew in breath and let it out in a long, soft whistle.

He drove to Beulah Yale's animal hospital and parked on a side street. All afternoon he had been thinking out his plan. The alley cat was backup. A motion picture might do it all.

I wish I were the Invisible Man, he thought.

Years before he had watched an old black-and-white motion picture by that name on television. A man drinks a secret formula and becomes invisible. . . .

To be *invisible*! Ashur placed his hands on the steering wheel and waited for them to vanish. The minutes dragged by without so much as the erasing of a hair or the evolution of a fingertip from dense to gauzy to transparent. His bare flesh—hands, wrists, and forearms—remained solidly visible, unaltered in shape and color and texture.

The Power had refused him.

Ashur grimaced ruefully. He had learned another hard lesson. Names of made-up people such as the Invisible Man lacked the magic to unlock the Power, just as nicknames or single names did. Someday he might figure out how to raid the world of fiction. For now, it was up to the cat.

"Let's call you Louey," Ashur said.

He knocked on the door of the Yale Animal Clinic. When no one responded, he knocked harder. Finally he shouted, "Open up. My cat is dying!"

The door opened, exposing a man's round face. "The hospital is closed," he said.

"Louey is dying," Ashur cried. "He's dying! Doctor Yale has to do something. She can save him. I know she can!"

"The hospital is closed," repeated the man, who looked more like a patient than an attendant. He had a bulldog's saggy jowls, which danced as he shook his head at Ashur. "Try again in a week, kid."

The door started to close, but Ashur's foot wedged it ajar.

"Can't I just leave Louey, please?"

"Stop shouting," the man hissed through taut lips.

"*Please?*" Ashur shouted.

"All right, if it'll shut you up," the man said. "Here, I'll take him. Give him to me."

Ashur held onto Louey and shouldered his way inside. "I want to be sure he has nice comfortable quarters. I want to see for myself."

"Keep your voice down, will you?" the man exhorted, and immediately changed tactics. He grinned and said with friendly humor, "You'll wake the guests. We run a nice, respectable place here. Couldn't be nicer at the Ritz. Room service, the works. Come in, come in so I can shut the door. I shouldn't be allowing this, you understand me, kid? I'm doing you a big favor. Don't give me trouble, okay? Take a fast look and leave. Louey'll love every minute. He's in good hands, so don't worry none."

They were standing in a wide reception room. A white counter ran its width to a corridor at either end. Ashur went to the left and was called back.

"Down there are the big cages for the big dogs," the man said. He spoke thickly, like an ex-boxer, and his tongue stumbled in his haste to get the words out. "The cages for the small dogs and cats are over here."

The corridor on the right was some thirty feet in length. Small steel cages stacked three-high lined most of one wall. The opposite wall was broken by three doors. From one of these stepped a man.

Ashur recognized him even though half his face was

wrapped in bandages. It was Hal of the overpass, the blonde Amazon's partner. Joe Louis's punch had done more than knock him senseless.

At the sight of Ashur, he stopped as if he had banged into a glass barrier. Cries like those of maddened crows tore through the bandages. His arms jiggled in excitement.

The big blonde appeared in the doorway. She wore dark sunglasses. Below the rims her face was a color chart of bruises. "Lance, are you out of your mind? What'd you let him in for? This is *the* kid!"

Lance turned white. "H-how could I know?" he complained. "He told me the cat was dying. I believed him. Look at it yourself."

"I have," the blonde said, her mouth working with anger. "It's probably dead already. Throw it someplace. Put the kid in the washing area while I telephone Masterson."

Lance nodded several times swiftly. Ashur's reputation as a fighter was printed on the faces of Hal and the blonde, and even Lance could read the message. His jaw set grimly, and he drew a pistol.

"Hands behind the neck, kid," he commanded. "You can't punch out a bullet, so let's enjoy the walk."

Ashur had made up his mind to not resist. Not before he had located Otto Lindt, anyway. He handed Louey to the blonde. She recoiled, and Louey landed lightly on the floor and scurried off. Lance started as if to give chase.

"Forget the cat, you idiot," the big blonde snapped. "Lock up the kid."

Ashur was marched back to the reception area, down the other corridor, and into the washing area.

Across from the door were two tiled cages, each large enough to be a horse's stall. One was empty, the other occupied. Normally big dogs such as Great Danes were kept there before they were bathed. Ashur had seen similar cages at his own veterinarian's in Dadesville.

Because of their large size and the bars on the doors, the cages in Dadesville reminded Ashur of cells in a prison. At the Yale Animal Clinic, this is what they were.

Seated inside one of the cages was a man.

He was well on in years. A white stubble covered his face, and his thin, gray hair strayed helter-skelter over his ears and forehead. His clothes were rumpled, as though he had worn them to bed and rolled in his sleep. And yet there was an undaunted look about him. He sat dead-still, a fortress of resolve within the degrading prison. Through the bars of the door of his cage, he silently contemplated Ashur.

"You can take the bench," Lance said.

Ashur picked up a metal bench from beside a raised bathtub and carried it into the empty cell.

"You'll be okay if you stay quiet," Lance said. He locked the cage and trudged out of the room.

A mirror on the far wall allowed Ashur to look into the other cage. Near the mirror was a window covered by two large white towels crudely but serviceably pinned together.

"Can you see London Bridge through that window?" Ashur asked the man in the next cage.

"Before they put the towel up, I had a fine broadside view," the man answered.

Ashur stared into the mirror unbelievingly. He did not know how he knew, but suddenly he did. His shocked, fascinated stare roved the gray-haired man. "You looked out the window Saturday night and you hummed 'London Bridge,' " Ashur said. "You're Otto Lindt, aren't you?"

"Yes, I am." The man rose from his chair and walked to the front of his cage. Gripping the bars of the door, he stared into the mirror at Ashur. "Who are you?"

"My name is Ashur Fine. I live in Florida."

"You're a long way from home, Ashur Fine."

"I came to speak to you."

"All the way from Florida, did you? You're asking me to believe that? Why, you're no more than sixteen or seventeen. I don't fool that easily. You're with them. You can save yourself a night on the bench by telling them my answer is still no."

"I'm not a spy. I don't have anyone to tell anything to," Ashur said. "I drove to Arizona because of my aunt. You saw who hit her."

"I don't know you or your aunt, young fellow."

"Remember last Saturday? A woman was about to serve you with a subpoena to appear as a witness in a traffic accident case. In Dadesville, near the Gold Star Hotel. She was mugged right in front of you. I want to know who did it. You didn't help her. You ran away. But you can identify the mugger."

"I remember a woman being knocked to the street outside the hotel. Yes, I saw who struck her. But I didn't run away."

"You didn't help her."

"I couldn't help myself. You can't help a lady in distress when you're being kidnapped by four men. Two of them flew me here in a rented four-seater that bounced when I sneezed."

The mystery was unraveling, but only a few inches. "Two of the men wore dark suits, didn't they?" Ashur said.

"All four of them wore dark suits. How'd you know that?"

"The other two stayed in Dadesville. I think they intended to kidnap me."

"Looks like they succeeded."

"Why did the same men want to kidnap us?" Ashur said. "I never heard of you before Saturday. We never met before today."

"You are full up with questions, boy," Otto Lindt said.

"I'll keep asking questions till I learn who mugged Aunt Ruth. They didn't have to knock her down to steal her money."

"You think it was an ordinary street crime? You really don't know what's going on, do you?"

"No, I don't. Tell me."

Otto Lindt bent forward, hands on the bars of the door, as if huddling with himself over whether to trust Ashur or not. After a long moment, he made his decision, saying, "Your aunt's mugging was a cover."

"What does that mean?"

"She happened to be in the right place at the wrong time. The four men in the dark suits wanted me, not your aunt's walk-around money. She just got caught in the middle."

"She wasn't mugged?" Ashur said skeptically. "I don't believe you."

"Believe what you will. The fact is, she had to be knocked out before they grabbed me. They couldn't allow a witness to my kidnapping. They took her money so that when she came to, she'd think that was the whole of it, that she'd been the victim of a street attack and nothing else had gone on. The men were after me and what I can do for them. Your aunt simply had the bad luck of finding me at the same time they did."

"They must want you awfully bad," Ashur said. "Whoever *they* are."

"It's a long story," Otto Lindt said.

"Tell me," Ashur replied. "This is one audience that won't walk out on you."

Otto Lindt dragged his chair to the front of the cell.

"I'm a dowser," he began in a low, earnest voice. "So was my daddy before me, and his daddy before him. It's an honest calling, but widely misunderstood. I've found water in Bermuda and Maine and Arizona with ol' Hawkeye—she's my number-one stick. I've helped police in seven states find stolen goods buried in lonely fields or under basement floors. I've even found a couple of oil wells in my time. But I refuse to dowse *that*."

He jabbed his finger as though piercing the towel-covered window across the room.

"I won't dowse London Bridge," he explained solemnly.

Ashur did not understand, but he did not interrupt.

Otto Lindt continued. "That isn't the only London Bridge—the others are still in London, of course. But it's an old one, built in eighteen thirty-one, and the last one of stone. Some years ago, an industrialist and a promoter had an idea. It was to turn this area, which was nothing but an unnamed stretch of sand, into a city. They needed a grand and spectacular attraction to lure home buyers into the desert. They flew to England and bought the bridge from the City of London, paying nearly two and a half million dollars for it. Everyone said they were crazy, but it proved to be worth every penny. The old bridge provided instant tradition for their instant city."

Otto Lindt paused as if disheartened by his thoughts. Then he said fiercely, "Two and a half million dollars is a handsome price. But today eleven of the granite stones in the bridge are worth many times that sum."

"Which eleven stones?" Ashur asked.

"That is the question," Otto Lindt said, "and it's why you and I are locked in cages meant for animals."

ELEVEN
THE SECRET
IN THE BRIDGE

"EACH one of those eleven stones is a small treasure chest," Otto Lindt said. "I was kidnapped to find them."

"They must be solid gold," Ashur said.

"What is *inside* them is as valuable. Did you ever hear of Conrad Hauser?"

"No."

"Not many people have. Hauser was a colonel in a special unit of the Nazi air force during the Second World War."

Otto Lindt pulled his chair closer to the door. He lowered his head slightly, thoughtfully, as though mentally arranging notes for a speech. After a few seconds he rested his hands in his lap and said:

"Hauser's job was cataloging the treasures stolen from conquered countries. Large artworks he turned over to high Nazi officials in Germany. But many smaller items—jewelry and stamps and coins—stuck to his fingers. As the Nazi armies were collapsing, he escaped to England with three trunkloads of jewels.

"Under a phony name, he set himself up as a watchmaker

in the village of Glassford and buried the jewels. Hauser wasn't greedy for himself. He wanted the treasure to finance the rebirth of Nazism. But through the nineteen fifties, anti-Nazi feeling was still strong. Hauser bided his time.

"Eventually the Nazis felt it safe to come out of hiding all around the world. Hauser met Roland Masterson, an American Nazi who lived by his wits. Masterson had connections of the right sort in the United States. He had peddled stolen paintings and artifacts in New York, California, and Rhode Island.

"The two men struck it off from the first. Within the year Hauser was confiding in Masterson. He told the American about the buried treasure.

"That was after London Bridge had been sold and it was being taken apart for shipment overseas to Arizona. Masterson saw in the bridge the means to smuggle the jewels out of England. He brought William Jenkins into the scheme. A master mason, Jenkins was in charge of removing the bridge's outer layer of granite stones.

"Jenkins hollowed out eleven of the stones. Inside them he cemented metal capsules containing the jewels. The stones were then patched expertly. They appeared untouched to anyone who didn't know what had been done.

"Two days after the work was completed, Conrad Hauser drowned in a boating accident—or so Roland Masterson told me. That reduced the number of shareholders in the treasure to two, Masterson and Jenkins."

Ashur interrupted. "How did Masterson and Jenkins plan to recover the eleven stones?"

"By stealing them before they reached Lake Havasu City," Otto Lindt answered, and resumed the tale.

"All the stones were numbered and brought ten thousand miles—across the Atlantic Ocean, through the Panama Canal, up the Pacific coast, and across the desert from California by truck. Masterson and Jenkins kept close tabs on the whereabouts of their eleven stones.

"They reached California when the largest shipment did. It filled sixty trucks. During the night, while the convoy of trucks was still at the port, they stole the truck with the eleven stones. Jenkins drove while Masterson followed in a camper, ready to make the transfer. Here, at the climax, the scheme came to grief.

"Jenkins had driven trucks in England, where vehicles travel on the left side of the road. He had never driven in America, on the right side. Piloting a heavy truck at night is tricky even for an experienced driver. Jenkins swerved to avoid a motorcyclist, tried to regain his lane, became confused, and ran off the road. The truck slammed head-on into a tree, killing him. Masterson fled in the camper, leaving the eleven stones at the wreck."

Ashur said, "How did you get involved?"

"Masterson tracked me to Los Angeles six months ago. He wanted me to dowse the bridge and locate the eleven stones."

"Is that possible?"

"I've tackled tougher jobs," Otto Lindt said. "But I wasn't going to get mixed up with Masterson, even for the million dollars he promised me. I stalled. I told him I needed a couple of days to think it over. From the way he looked at me, I knew I'd better lose myself in a hurry. I went as far as the country allowed, to Dadesville. I figured I was safe till the automobile accident, when the policeman took my name and address as a witness. The rest I've told you."

"I don't understand how the four men in dark suits knew you'd come to Dadesville," Ashur said.

"Roland Masterson, as I mentioned, has connections of the right sort—in the underworld," Otto Lindt said. "What I was afraid might happen, did happen. Some dishonest Dadesville official noticed my name on the accident report and informed Masterson."

Ashur still had questions. He said, "If each stone was numbered before it was shipped from London, why doesn't Masterson know where the eleven are?"

"William Jenkins kept the eleven numbers to himself," Otto Lindt replied. "It was his insurance against being double-crossed. Furthermore, the numbers were removed from all the stones when the bridge was assembled here."

"I don't know why Masterson needs a dowser," Ashur said. "There are all types of machines for detecting hidden substances."

"Right you are," Otto Lindt said. "But they'd attract attention too early. The user would have to get up on the tuna tower of a boat as she floats under the bridge. Masterson knows I can pick out the stones without going near the bridge."

"How can you do that?" Ashur asked.

"I'll tell you true—I'm the best. It's in the blood. I've found water and hidden objects a dozen times just by running a branch over a map of the land. I'd do the same with a map of the bridge."

"Suppose you located the eleven stones," Ashur said. "What then?"

"Masterson is on top of that. The four men in the dark suits are scuba divers. William Jenkins put all the jewels into stones on the outside surface of the same arch. When Masterson knows which of the five arches is the right one, he'll mark every outside stone. Then he'll blow enough of the bridge for those stones to fall off. The scuba divers will pick up the marked stones under water and bring them to a boat waiting in the lake. It sounds a good deal harder than it really is."

To Ashur it sounded impossible. Yet Otto Lindt had talked of the feat with easy, matter-of-fact confidence. He made dowsing, blowing up the bridge, and recovering the jewels under water seem commonplace acts.

Lance, the man who had admitted Ashur and Louey to the animal hospital, entered the room. He took the gun from his belt and unlocked Ashur's cage.

"Step lively," he said. "Mr. Masterson wants to talk to you."

At last, Ashur thought. Whatever lay ahead, he had to face Masterson sooner or later. Masterson could explain why the capture of a sixteen-year-old boy had been worth the extraordinary outlay of effort, time, and risk.

They were gathered in the office. Hal and the blonde Amazon were seated in front of the broad curved desk.

Behind the desk sat a handsome man in his sixties,

94

suavely barbered and expensively tailored. He rubbed the palms of his hands together as if drying them of problems.

"This is the kid, Mr. Masterson," Lance said.

"Sit," Roland Masterson said amiably, and studied Ashur with dark, untelling eyes. "You're quite a lad, I understand. What's your name?"

"Ashur Fine."

"You eluded two of my men in Dadesville, and you nearly killed Hal with your fists," Masterson said. "I need Hal. He's a wizard with explosives. He can blow a bank safe and never tip a picture on the wall."

"He tried to kidnap me," Ashur said.

"And what about Mabel? She's a black belt in judo and three styles of karate. She's beaten men, beaten them till their wives and girlfriends winced with shame. But her best wasn't good enough to handle you."

"She kicks like a mule," Ashur conceded.

"Then you outwitted Boola, and that's like winning the Triple Crown in one horse race. Boola called from West Gulfport, Louisiana. You rigged it so that the police believed she and two of my divers came to West Gulfport to recover a stolen jewel, the Anderson diamond. It was found in a pipe under a sink in an old factory. Boola can't figure how you knew it was there, but you did. You framed her and took off."

"She tried to kidnap me, too," Ashur said stiffly.

"You outsmart kidnappers. You fight like a grizzly bear. You turn the tables on the cleverest woman I know. And there is your piano playing. It stopped traffic in a shopping center. You're a most unusual boy. Who are you?"

"Ashur Fine. I told you."

Masterson pressed against the high leather back of his chair, his expressionless eyes never leaving Ashur's face. He rocked thoughtfully. "I shall rephrase the question," he said, the words hissing like sword strokes. "*What* are you?"

Ashur shook his head in a manner he hoped conveyed innocent puzzlement. "I have a gift," he said, as though referring to a knack for buttoning his shirt.

"Peddle that somewhere else," Mabel jeered. "You broke Hal's jaw with a six-inch punch, and you did what no one else ever came close to doing—put me away. You're unreal."

"Are you unreal?" Masterson goaded.

"Why did you try to kidnap me?" Ashur countered.

Masterson smiled. "So Otto Lindt told you. You should never have been put in the same room. Well, there's no harm done."

"He told me about the jewels in the bridge," Ashur retorted. "I know why one of your divers hit my aunt. But why did you go to so much trouble to capture me?"

"I'm surprised," Masterson said. "You should have figured that out by yourself. So, Ruth Owens is your aunt. We guessed some such relationship. Holding you prisoner was the best way to guarantee her silence, just in case she was conscious after being hit and saw us kidnap Otto Lindt."

"You went to a lot of trouble for nothing," Ashur said. "Otto Lindt's kidnapping was perfectly disguised. My aunt believes she was mugged and that Otto Lindt ran away out of fright. You shouldn't have bothered with me."

Masterson made no reply for several seconds. When he spoke, his words were edged with a strange, dreamy quality. "I'm glad we bothered," he said. "I've grown exceptionally fond of you, professionally speaking. You drove more than twenty-five hundred miles by yourself to find whoever hit your aunt, isn't that right?"

"I'd drive another twenty-five hundred," Ashur said.

"You don't have to. I'm responsible. It's between you and me," Masterson said, and added ceremonially, "If you wish satisfaction, I await your pleasure. What shall it be: pistols, swords, karate?"

"Whatever you choose."

"Good! Shall we make it . . . jewels?" Masterson turned on the smile again and glanced around the room. "There are quite enough of them for everyone. A boy who knew exactly where Otto Lindt had been taken—to this dot on a road map—is worth having as a partner. Now there is the riddle. Tell me, how *did* you know that we'd taken Lindt to Lake Havasu City?"

"I'm good at road maps," Ashur said.

The quip nudged Masterson's lips into a genuine smile. "Count yet another talent," he said. "Humor."

"Funny, funny," Mabel scoffed. "Get rid of the kid. He's spooky."

"You think with your biceps, my dear Mabel," Masterson said. "Consider what we have. A problem: jewels that we can't locate. A solution: a young man with the gift of extrasensory perception. He knew that a diamond was hidden in a pipe in a West Gulfport glass factory. What our young friend can find in a metal pipe, he can find in granite stones."

Masterson had it all wrong. Nonetheless, Ashur thought, his readiness to accept the supernatural as a practicable tool was unsettling.

"We don't need the kid," Mabel persisted.

Hal lent her support by stamping his foot.

"It seems that I'm to be overruled," Masterson said. He deadpanned the remark, and those untelling eyes gave no clue as to whether he was jesting. "I put it to you, Ashur. Do you care to have a million dollars before you are old enough to vote?"

"What will happen to Otto Lindt?"

"Nothing," Masterson said. "When the jewels are safely ours, he'll be released."

"If I refuse to help? What becomes of me?"

"You will be set free with Lindt," Masterson answered. "And your aunt in Dadesville will not be harmed. I'll wager that worried you. Afraid we'd torture her till you agreed to help us, eh? Nothing of the kind." He made a little gesture of dismissal. "Now, how say you? Are you in?"

Masterson's assurance of goodwill was not meant to fool anyone, Ashur realized. On the contrary, the thin veil of denial made the threat of harm more forceful than if it had been stated nakedly.

Ashur rose and walked slowly around the room as though considering the offer. When he came near the desk and could look down on Masterson, he stopped.

"Yes, I'm with you, but not for a million dollars," he said. "I was raised on the Ten Commandments, and I've never broken them. If I'm to start now, let the reward be worth the sin. Say, half the jewels?"

Roland Masterson's face darkened fleetingly. "Say, ten percent."

"Twenty-five percent."

"Can you find the eleven stones?"

"I have the power."

Masterson silenced Mabel, Hal, and Lance with a slight, murderous lidding of his eyes.

"Twenty-five percent and done," he said.

He held out his hand. Ashur took it and they shook, grinning at each other.

TWELVE
ATTILA

IT was immediately evident that the partnership was no more than skin-deep. As they clasped hands, Ashur felt the abiding distrust of people in Masterson.

"We'll have to keep you here overnight, I'm afraid," Masterson said with a proper dash of regret. "I'll be back in the morning. We'll start work then. Mabel and Lance and Hal will see to your comfort."

Having summed up the way it was to be, he smiled at everyone and took his leave.

"We'd better watch the kid in shifts," Lance said to Mabel. "You take the first, then Hal, then me. Three hours each?"

Mabel nodded and lowered herself into Beulah Yale's desk chair. "Give me the gun and get Attila."

Lance surrendered the weapon. He left the room and returned leading a Doberman pinscher. The animal went knowingly to the side of the desk. It turned in a tight circle and lay down, all sleekness and bound fury.

"Meet our darling Attila. He's so adoooorable!" Mabel cooed in silly baby tones. She stroked the black dog on the neck. "Lance trained him, but I can give all the lovely commands."

Lance said, "If you want me, I'll be sacked out in surgery."

Mabel tossed him a coy, beddy-bye wave with her stalwart hand. She noticed Ashur watching the gun.

"Don't try for it," she advised. "Attila looks like a dear, but he obeys three interesting commands. The first gets him ready, the third quiets him down." She shot Ashur a sly and wicked grin. "The *second* is the *most* interesting. It makes him tear people apart."

"Is that a nice way to welcome your new partner?" Ashur said.

"Masterson calls you partner. To the rest of us, you're trouble with a capital T."

Ashur glanced at his watch. He had to give Lance a few minutes to settle down in surgery. "Does Vance work for Dr. Yale?"

"It's *Lance*—Timothy Lance," Mabel corrected. "He'll work at the hospital till the time comes to use his boat and—" She caught herself. She flung back her broad shoulders and glared at Ashur. "You talk too much. Everything you do is too much."

"Mind if I sleep?" Ashur inquired. "It won't take long. I sleep fast."

Ashur put his head back and closed his eyes. He had foxed Mabel into revealing Lance's full name. To obtain the three commands that controlled Attila, he had only to say, I wish I were Timothy Lance.

He was on the verge of summoning the Power when he

101

realized the pitfall. What would happen if Lance came back into the room and faced himself in another human? Ashur dared not chance it.

Besides, he didn't have to know the three commands. There was another way.

He opened his eyes and sat up in his chair. "Suppose you're not the only one who knows the commands," he said to Mabel. "Suppose I know them, too."

"You're bluffing," Mabel retorted.

Ashur looked at Attila. *Get ready to attack.*

Attila sat up alertly.

The gun rose and pointed at Ashur's heart. "H-how'd you do that?" Mabel demanded.

"I imitated Timothy Lance," Ashur said. "Soundless impersonations are a specialty. I do a great Charlie Chaplin and other stars of the silent films. Want to hear?"

"Shut your mouth," Mabel snapped.

"You wouldn't shoot me," Ashur said. "You wouldn't dare. Not here. Not at night. The police would be at the door in five minutes. A dog is different. Barking and snarling are normal sounds in an animal hospital."

"Dog or gun, it doesn't matter to me which way you get it," Mabel said.

"What if *I* gave the command to attack?" Ashur asked.

"Attila would go for you, not for me. He knows me," Mabel said. "He'd chew your head off. That's what he's trained to do."

She looked at Attila. The dog was staring at her with pitiless attention.

"Ease down," she commanded.

Attila ignored her. He sat as motionless as iron. He was primed, and he waited for the command that would trigger him.

"I gave the first command," Ashur said. "I doubt that Attila will obey the second command from anyone else."

"Ease down," Mabel repeated in an edgy, high key.

The Doberman remained rigid, muscles tensed, his bloodthirsty gaze fixed on her face.

Mabel suddenly seemed on the verge of a complete physical and mental collapse. "Oh, lordy, no," she breathed.

Ashur shielded his mouth. When Mabel looked at him again, he moved his lips silently, as if forming the second command, the command to attack.

Mabel broke. "Please, kid, don't," she pleaded with hoarse and choking desperation. "Don't."

At the back of the room, Hal began to whimper through his casing of bandages.

Slowly and deliberately, Mabel laid the gun on the desk. "Take it," she gasped.

Ashur put the gun in his belt. *Ease down.*

The dog relaxed and settled onto the carpet.

"Let's go to the washing area, all of us," Ashur said. "And no noise."

Once in the big room, Ashur gestured toward Otto Lindt. "Unlock the cage."

"Lance has the key," Mabel said.

Ashur didn't really need the key. He had the Power. He had simply to wish he were Harry Houdini, the great American escape artist, and pick the lock.

Pressing hard on that thought was a wiser one. Don't

show off the Power unless there is no choice.

"I'll be back with the key in a minute," he said to Otto Lindt.

Attila moved with him to the door. Ashur paused and bent slightly. *Watch them.*

Attila barked once, his sharp black head snapping viciously. As he lapsed into vigilant growls, his fangs shone whiter than white. Hal and Mabel froze.

Ashur stole into the surgery room, leaned over the table, and pushed the gun under Lance's chin. Eyes rolling in terror, Lance went quietly to the washing area.

Ashur lifted his ring of keys and freed Otto Lindt. He locked Mabel, Hal, and Lance in one cage and Attila in the other.

"I can put the dog in with you," he told Mabel. "Or would you rather talk to me?"

Mabel decided that she'd rather talk than have Attila for a roommate. She knew very little, however.

Masterson was staying at the Wayside Inn on Harrison Boulevard, a mile south of the animal hospital, she said. He was registered under his real name and not Roger Moreland, the name he'd used when he'd sought out Hal to blow the bridge.

Being Hal's wife, she had been drawn deeper and deeper into the plot. "Masterson figured my black belts might come in handy," she said. "He didn't foresee a teenage crazy."

Except that Roland Masterson went by other names, Mabel could add nothing important to what Otto Lindt had told him about the plot to recover the jewels. Ashur believed her.

She was too frightened of Attila to lie.

Ashur assured her that she had done well and that Attila would remain in the other cage. Then he tidied up.

He wiped the gun with his handkerchief and placed it in a cabinet beside a container of flea-and-tic dip. He switched off the light and pulled the towels from the room's one window.

Louey lay napping beside a bag of dry cereal in the other wing of the hospital. Ashur released the little alley cat outdoors. "Thanks for helping me crash the party," he said, bestowing a farewell pat.

With Otto Lindt he walked to the station wagon. Overhead the immense night sky shone with a bumper crop of stars.

"I need a lift to Dadesville," Otto Lindt said.

"You'll have it," Ashur said, "in a day or so. I have some unfinished business in Lake Havasu City."

"Revenge is the lousiest of motives," Otto Lindt offered quietly.

"I came to find the man who hit my Aunt Ruth," Ashur said. "It was one of the dark-suits. I'm not going back to Dadesville before I find out which one."

"Was your aunt badly hurt?"

"No," Ashur admitted. "It's the principle."

"Principle, is it? Don't hide behind principle because you don't like the truth," Otto Lindt said.

"I've told you the truth."

"The truth is," Otto Lindt said, "you've had your revenge. Masterson is finished. He can't go after the jewels. He doesn't know whom we'll tell. The bridge was his biggest score. You

105

smashed it to twigs. Do you want to chase after him the rest of your life just to find out which scuba diver threw a punch at your aunt?"

Ashur considered the question. What did it matter now who had knocked down Aunt Ruth?

In his righteous anger he had vowed to take revenge, but suddenly a line that Aunt Ruth once quoted came into his head: "What begins in anger, ends in shame."

Aunt Ruth and Otto Lindt were right. It took more strength to yield to truth than to stand on principle.

"There is always a better way to do something," Otto Lindt said.

Ashur did not reply immediately. Almost without being conscious of it, he had already begun his "better way." He had stripped the towels from the washing area window so that the room could be seen from the street.

His mind strung together the rest of the pieces that would put Masterson and his gang behind bars. When the last detail was tied in place, he smiled with devilish pleasure.

"It's time we reported Masterson to the police," he said.

The desk sergeant at police headquarters listened patiently to the blurted story. When Ashur was done, the sergeant summoned a Detective Dawson.

Dawson ushered Ashur and Otto Lindt into a small bare office. The most prominent features were two desks, and two trash baskets filled with empty styrene coffee cups. The detective looked as worn out as the room. He wrote down their names and addresses.

Ashur had to repeat the story he had told to the desk sergeant. "About an hour ago," he said, "we were walking past the Yale Animal Clinic on Delano Street. We heard some-one calling for help. Through the window we made out two men and a woman inside a large cage. They said a man named Roland Masterson had robbed them and locked them up."

The detective listened absently. He alternately stared into space and doodled stars on a pad as if he didn't believe two words.

"Did they say who this Roland Masterson is?" he asked.

"They only met him this afternoon at the bar in the Way-side Inn," Ashur replied.

"They said he was a really smooth talker," Otto Lindt put in.

"We'll check it out," the detective muttered wearily. He studied Ashur and Otto Lindt. "You two are a long way from Dadesville, Florida."

"Ashur drove out to get me," Otto Lindt said. "I don't like to fly. I like my feet close to the ground. I'm a dowser."

That makes as much sense as anything, the detective's expression seemed to say. He rubbed at the weariness in his eyes. "Where can I reach you in Lake Havasu City?"

"I checked out of my hotel at noon," Otto Lindt said. "We'll stay wherever you tell us."

"Suit yourselves," the detective said. "I finish at eight in the morning. Be here at seven."

Out on the street, Otto Lindt was all smiles. "This I have to see."

"Me, too," Ashur said.

They saw it an hour later. They were seated in the station wagon at the Wayside Inn when two uniformed policemen drove up to the office. Despite his doubts, Detective Dawson had followed procedure.

The fact that the police were at the motel meant that Hal, Mabel, and Lance had been found locked in the cage at the Yale Animal Clinic.

Within ten minutes, Roland Masterson was led from his ground-floor room to the patrol car.

"Praise the police!" Ashur exclaimed. "It's working!"

"We'll know for sure at seven o'clock tomorrow morning," Otto Lindt said.

THIRTEEN
THE COMPUTER

THEY took a room at the Wayside Inn and awoke with the broadening light of dawn.

None of the restaurants in Lake Havasu City served breakfast before seven o'clock. To kill time until their appointment with Detective Dawson, they strolled across London Bridge.

Ashur said, "Do you think Masterson could have blown an arch of the bridge and recovered the jewels?"

"Why not? He put together a team of experts," Otto Lindt replied. "He just made two mistakes—you and me. He'll never understand us or anyone else who isn't a slave to greed."

Otto Lindt shook his head sadly. His hair flopped out every which way, for he had not used a comb since being kidnapped in Dadesville. But beneath the wild gray mop lay a keen and sensitive mind, a mind that prized honesty and the honor of a dying profession. It would be hard to separate from such a man.

They had stopped walking and were standing side by side. Otto Lindt peered down at the channel as though remembering the people for whom he had found water in dusty farmlands and rockbound coastal islands.

As for Ashur, he was suddenly blinded to everything save the riches hidden somewhere beneath his feet. He alone could go straight to the eleven stones. He knew a name.

To pinpoint the jewels, he had merely to wish he were the dead William Jenkins, the London stonemason who had hidden them.

Masterson had failed because he couldn't replace William Jenkins. Ashur didn't need to. He had the Power. For the rest of it, he had Masterson's plan.

The idea struck him with the force of a revelation.

He staggered backward a half-step, shocked at this greed. For the first time he truly feared the Power growing in him. Could it take over his soul, decaying all that was selfless and good?

A momentary panic seized him. He held up his hands as if he might see evil coursing in his veins and by hardening his will stop it.

Otto Lindt glanced at him questioningly.

"It's ten to seven," Ashur uttered hastily, embarrassed. "We'd better be moving."

In front of police headquarters, Otto Lindt said, "If we keep to our story, we're fine. Masterson and the others won't dare mention us. If they do, they're confessed kidnappers."

Detective Dawson was pacing his office. At the sight of Ashur and Otto Lindt, he swallowed the last of his coffee and flipped the cup into the wastebasket.

"We've got a dandy here," he announced. "It's going to take days to straighten this out. There are warrants outstanding in five states on Roland Masterson, alias Roger Moreland, alias

Ron Mason, alias pick-a-name. There is one on Harold Wells, a safecracker who jumped bail in Utah last year. The other two locked up in the animal hospital, Timothy Lance and Mabel Wells, are clean."

"You didn't waste time," Otto Lindt commented.

"Credit the computer age," Dawson replied. "In a few minutes we can get a feedout on a lawbreaker in any of the countries participating in the Security-A network."

He sat down in front of his typewriter.

"I'll need your statement, Mr. Lindt," he said. "Sergeant Kaplan will take yours, Mr. Fine, at the first desk. Then you're both free to go."

In the large outer room, Sergeant Kaplan had already rolled a triplicate form into her typewriter. Ashur repeated the made-up story that had convinced Detective Dawson yesterday—how he and Otto Lindt had looked through a window of the animal hospital and seen people locked in a cage.

Ashur deliberately kept the account brief, as Otto Lindt had suggested. The simpler their statements, the more closely they would agree.

Afterward, Detective Dawson walked with them to the parking area.

"It's one nutty business," he mused. "What were they all doing in the Yale Animal Clinic in the first place? They won't say anything except to their lawyers. Maybe Dr. Yale can help us, or maybe she's involved herself. We'll know when she gets back to town."

Otto Lindt beamed at Ashur and shifted the subject. He got the detective to talk about the police computer. Ashur didn't listen. His attention had strayed to the bridge. From where he stood, he saw the five arches clearly against the heat-dried landscape.

The searing desert sun had bleached more than a century of London grime from the stones. Against the unlikely backdrop of palm trees and beaches, the bridge stretched elegantly, an Old World monument of unique and splendid dignity.

It's more beautiful and more precious than money, Ashur thought. Let the jewels lie in it forever.

He was untempted and unchanged. The knowledge came to him as a great joy and a greater relief. With all the gladness of his heart he offered up thanks. The Power had not corrupted him.

The attack of greed an hour earlier, the temptation to sacrifice the historic structure, had been conquered. The Power belonged to him, not he to it. The Power was his to wield as *he* chose, an instrument for good and not evil.

And, never to be forgotten, it was also his shield against the one terrible, constant danger. For beyond the hot, blank Arizona sky lay the inescapable showdown with Methuselah, a creature so old he had no age. Ashur knew he must choose the time and place for the encounter with the giant elephant, and prepare himself well.

Suddenly Otto Lindt, who had been chatting with Detective Dawson, exclaimed excitedly, "Ashur! Did you hear that?"

"No," the boy admitted. He felt a perfect fool. "I was daydreaming."

"Tell him about the new computer," Otto Lindt urged the detective.

"I understand it's twenty years ahead of its time," the detective said. "There are only two in existence. The police department will get one next month to put on the roof. The other will be set outdoors in Juneau, Alaska. The idea is to find out how the models hold up in extremes of hot and cold."

The detective did his best to relate the marvels of the new computer. His knowledge of the subject was slight and made his description unclear and boring.

Ashur pretended to listen while his mind wandered impatiently. He yearned to get out of the blazing sun, climb into the air-conditioned station wagon, and drive with Otto Lindt to Dadesville.

"Imagine," the detective was saying, "a machine that can think by itself!"

"But can it find water?" Otto Lindt joshed.

"I'll be happy if it can find where Sergeant Kaplan hides the coffee cups," the detective said. He swung his arms and slapped his palms in front of him. "It's been a long night. Let's go home."

He wished them a safe trip back to Florida, and they wished him good luck with the strange case at the Yale Animal Clinic.

Ashur had the station wagon moving before realization caught up with him.

"Blast me!" he swore out loud.

He braked to a standstill, stalling the engine, and flung open the door.

"Back in a minute!" he said to the astonished Otto Lindt.

He hurried down the row of cars, his head pounding with

a frenzied rhythm: I nearly missed it! I nearly missed it! I nearly missed it!

He stopped alongside the detective's scarred and faded two-door and gestured with both hands.

The detective let go of the ignition key and lowered the window. "What is it? Forget something?"

"The new computer, the one that's twenty years ahead of its time," Ashur said.

"Yes?"

A slow smile crept over Ashur's face. "Does it have a name?"